JOURNEY THRO

Higher Ways Series Book 2

© M.C. Spencer, July 2016

Small Pond Press
Box 637 Blackfalds
Alberta Canada
T0M 0J0

smallpond@telus.net

SMALL POND
PRESS

Journey Through Fire and Smoke

First Edition
Published by Small Pond Press

SMALL POND
PRESS

For you, God, tested us; you refined us like silver. You brought us into prison and laid burdens on our backs ... we went through fire and water, but you brought us to a place of abundance.

Psalm 66: 10-12

Chapter One

"Prince Eghan?"

He turned his head with a jerk at the sound of his name. Being addressed by his formal title was not as familiar as it had once been.

Silhas, the king's advisor, raised his eyebrows. "Shall I announce you?"

Eghan took a deep breath and faced the huge carved doors again. Beyond them lay the great hall, filled now, Eghan knew, with every nobleman allowed in his father's court. They were all waiting for him.

Khalwyd, his guardian, touched his arm. When he turned, the man placed a long shape wrapped in soft deer skins in his hands. He handed the skins back to Khalwyd, then nodded to Silhas. The doors swung open.

Before he could count the beats of his pounding heart, he was dropping to one knee, both arms extended, the sword of the House of Lhin resting on his open palms. He bowed his head before his father, King Gherin Lhin. As his knee touched the floor, Eghan felt the heavy sword being taken and strong hands on his arms, pulling him to his feet.

Then he was caught into a tight embrace. He wrapped his arms around his father and tried to keep the tears from coming. When he stepped back and looked into the king's face, they spilled over.

Gherin Lhin beamed at him, tears streaking his face as well. "Eghan." His voice choked and he had to clear his throat. "You have grown."

Eghan felt the grip tighten on his arms.

"A boy disappeared and a man has returned in his place." He pulled him close again. "I thank God you are safe."

Though Eghan knew that his father had come to faith in The One True God, the king's words stunned him and when he spoke his voice was husky with emotion. "He has kept me, Father, and blessed me, in spite of everything."

Gherin released him and took the sword from his servant. He pulled it from its sheath and held it high. Eghan heard people gasp and whisper as the jewels caught the light and the polished-metal flashed. Looking down at him, the king raised his voice so the everyone in the hall would hear. "Has this weapon drawn blood, by your hand?"

Eghan swallowed and answered in an equally loud voice. "It has, Sire, the blood of Duke Malnar, enemy to the Lhinian throne and enemy to his own people."

Lowering the weapon, the king placed it on his open palms and looked down at it. "Then you have proven yourself worthy of it, Prince Eghan Lhin." He looked up. "And one day it will belong only to you." The king handed the weapon back to his servant, then smiled and shouted to the people, "Long live Prince Eghan!"

The crowd erupted, chanting, "Long live the Prince. Long live Prince Eghan."

The king put his arm around Eghan's shoulders. "Welcome home, son!" He propelled him forward. "You must be weary, and anxious to get out of those rags, no doubt."

Eghan looked down at himself. He had dressed in the best Alingan clothing he could find before arriving at his father's castle, but to any Lhinian they would seem like the rags of a peasant. He grinned. "And a hot bath?"

Gherin smiled back. "That would be appropriate."

They walked together into the private apartments where Eghnan had spent all but this last year of his life. In his room, servants were scurrying in and out behind a tall screen, filling a tub with steaming water and laying out clothes on a huge bed. Eghan stood in the doorway and watched for a moment, then stepped slowly over the threshold. He felt awkward, uncomfortable. This was his room but he felt like a foreigner in it.

A servant bowed in front of him. "The bath is ready, my prince. Is there anything else you wish?"

Eghan stared, then came to himself. "No. No, that will be all." The servant stepped back.

The king sat in a chair by the window as Eghan moved behind the screen, peeled off his clothes and lowered himself into the hot water. He stretched out and let himself relax.

"Aaaah, you don't know how many times I have dreamed of this over the past few months."

"I am glad to hear it." Eghan could hear the smile in his father's voice. "I thought perhaps you would be completely out of the habit, having lived with the Alingans."

Eghan chuckled. "It is a habit I will welcome falling back into, Father." He watched as the servant poured another bucket of water into the tub. "But there may be others that will not come so easily."

"Such as?"

"Being waited on hand and foot. Even Uncle Adlair's house had no servants."

The king snorted. "Adlair always was a peasant at heart."

Eghan noted the hard edge to his father's voice, but ignored it. He looked at his hands, still thickened from the work he had done in his uncle's house. "When I lived with him I chopped wood, hauled water, worked in the fields, even cleaned the stables."

Gherin's voice showed his amazement. "You did the work of a slave?"

"Yes. If I did not work, I did not eat."

"Outrageous!"

Eghan chuckled again at the shock in his father's voice. "It is in accordance with The Book, Father, and to be truthful, I rather liked the work, once I got used to it. Being treated like a prince now seems almost wrong."

"Put on some descent clothes, sleep long in your own bed and you will feel more like yourself again."

"Perhaps."

The servant stooped to pick up the Alingan garments. Eghan lifted his hand and said quietly, "Clean them and bring them back to me." The servant bowed and left the room. Eghan finished washing, stepped out of the tub and wrapped a drying cloth around his waist. He walked to the bed, pulled on a pair of fine breeches and reached for the tunic.

Gherin stood to his feet. "Who has dared to strike you?"

The sound of his father's voice made Eghan shiver. He had forgotten about the scars on his back. He turned as he pulled the tunic over his head. "An Alingan soldier. He knew me only as a peasant who stopped him from beating a child. If it had not been for Khalwyd, I would have more than just these four stripes. Some died at the whipping posts in Alinga territory. Malnar's concept of justice was brutal."

"Then the earth is well rid of him."

Eghan frowned. "I am not sure we are rid of him, Father."

"But he is dead, at your hand, so you have told me. Tell me more of how you defeated him."

Eghan was silent for a moment. When he spoke his voice was low. "I had little to do with it. The Duke's defeat came at the hands of the Alingans themselves, farmers and villagers and a handful of soldiers. They were helped by the Mountain Huntsmen and, most of all, by the mercy of our God." Eghan described the last battle, the earthquake that destroyed Malnar's castle, the timely arrival of Eghan's uncle and an army of Huntsmen. "I was there only as a witness," he said.

"A witness has no blood on his hands."

Eghan's voice dropped another notch. "Malnar's blood is on my hands, and on the sword of the House of Lhin, because I had no choice. He would have killed Nara."

"The Alingan Princess."

Eghan nodded. "The rightful heir to the Alingan throne."

"I see." The king's eyes narrowed. "Then this princess now owes you a heavy debt."

"A debt that will never be called," Eghan responded quickly.

"Such a debt can be a political advantage, Eghan, one not to be tossed aside."

"I count Nara as a friend now, Father, not as a political adversary."

"I see." Eghan noted the stiffness in his father's voice.

"As Queen she will be our ally, and I hope you will be willing to treat with her people."

"And is she worthy to be queen?"

Eghan hesitated. "She is more than worthy. Yet ..."

The king did not respond for some time. When he broke the silence his voice was soft. "Yet you wish she were not queen, of the Alinga."

Eghan looked into his father's eyes. "I would give anything to keep her from that throne."

"And is there anything that will keep her from it?"

Eghan dropped his eyes and shook his head. "No. It is her place."

Gherin watched his son's face closely. "And your place is here. But you seem to have more than a passing interest in this Alingan princess."

Eghan was silent for a while. "At first I hated her, because she was Alingan. But the more I let the Lord work, the more those feelings changed."

"That seems to be His main business, changing the hearts of His people."

Eghan raised his head. "Silhas told me how you yielded to Him."

Gherin smiled but there was sadness in his eyes. "Silhas will never know how close he came to the gallows. Did he tell you he called me a fool to my face?" The king laughed. "Imagine the boldness of the man! My rage very nearly kept me from admitting he was right, but yes, I finally did yield." Gherin leaned forward. "And when I did, I began to realize how foolish I have been. We have made many changes in a very short time, Eghan. Most of the people are responding well. Many have become believers, but there are struggles too. I pray every day for wisdom to lead in the way He directs."

Eghan smiled. "It is so good to hear you talk about Him, Father. Knowing Him has become important to me over the past few months. It is good to know He is important to you as well."

"His grace and love have often overwhelmed me in these days past." Gherin lowered his voice. "He showed me how empty I was, how cold I had become, especially since your mother died." He stood, reached out and touched Eghan's arm. "We have lost many years, Eghan. We cannot go back, but I hope we can truly become a father and son in the days ahead."

"There is nothing I want more, Father." Eghan's eyes filled. His father had never spoken to him this way before. They embraced and, for the first time in many months, Eghan felt entirely safe. It was a long time before his father pushed him gently away. "The servants have been preparing for your arrival for days. There is a great feast laid out in the hall. Are you hungry?

"Famished."

Gherin laughed. "At least some things have not changed. I fear we will have to send our hunters out more often, now that you are home." He squeezed his shoulder. "Come. The table is set. We will talk more as we feast."

Eghan's mind whirled with questions as he walked with his father through the corridors of his grand castle and into the hall where the feast was laid out on long tables. It seemed like years since he had left here, been taken unconscious from his home, but it was just over one year since that day.

So much had changed. What place would he have now, in his father's house? His mind whirled but his tongue stayed silent. Old patterns are hard to break and Eghan was not accustomed to sharing his thoughts with his father. As he followed the king into the hall he scanned the throng of people to see if Khalwyd and Silhas were among them. He spotted them near the far doors and waved them closer, noting as they came that they too had bathed and changed their clothing.

The king smiled when he saw them. "Khalwyd, Silhas. Forgive my rudeness. You have brought my son back to me and I have not even acknowledged your presence." He extended his hand to each of them. "Welcome, and thank you. I can assure you that you will both be well rewarded."

Eghan stared. He had never in his life heard his father speak that way, not as a king to his subjects, but as a man to his friends. He caught Khalwyd's eye and noticed the amazement there as well.

Gherin grinned at his son, as though he had read Eghan's thoughts. "You are not the only one who has changed, Eghan." He grasped the back of Eghan's neck. "Come. We have a feast to devour and so much to talk about." As they took their places the king asked his first question. "How is that brother-in-law of mine? I expected him to be with you."

"Uncle Adlair said to give you warm greetings, Father, but felt it best to remain with Nar ... with the Alingans, for a while. He promised to come as soon as he is able."

Gherin nodded, a look of concern in his eyes as he turned to Silhas. "I hope Adlair knows he is welcome?"

Silhas smiled. "Yes, Sire, and he is anxious to meet with you, brother to brother."

"And I with him. Though I may be tempted to throw him in my dungeon for a time, for kidnapping my son."

Eghan peered into his father's face, relieved to see the king was not serious. Still, he felt he had to speak. "Uncle Adlair saved my life, Father, in more ways than one. And he was good to me. He was like a ..." He stopped, suddenly hesitant to say what was in his mind and his heart.

"Like a father?"

Gherin's eyes were piercing and Eghan thought he saw a shadow there, but he nodded.

"Yes, like a father."

"All the more reason to thank him."

Eghan's tension broke as the dark look in his father's eyes faded. He smiled as Gherin gripped his shoulder, turned to the throng around them and shouted. "My son is home! Let the feast begin!"

The people burst into cheers and music erupted from the outer court.

As others gathered at the table Eghan stared at the meat, vegetables, bread and fruit piled high on large platters. He thought of the weeks spent in caves on the fringes of Alinga territory when they had little more than a bit of bread in their stomachs and some days not even that. Taking a large apple in his hand, he stared at it for a moment, breathed in the smell of it, then took a huge bite. The crisp tart pulp exploded in his mouth and he closed his eyes, imagining the trees throughout the valley, bent with the weight of fruit at harvest time. He imagined himself handing an apple to Nara, watching her as she savored it. He imagined her smile. Opening his eyes, he stared at the fruit in his hand and a sadness swelled up inside him. Nara was not here, celebrating. Nor would she ever be. She was on the other side of the mountains in that barren, inhospitable land, perhaps going hungry so others could eat.

Eghan raised his eyes to see Khalwyd take an apple in his hand and address the king, though his eyes were on Eghan. "Sire, are your cellars still full of fruit so good?"

Gherin cocked his head at the guardian. "You know how bountiful our orchards are, Khalwyd. Yes, there is plenty of fruit to be had. The harvest was ample this year, as always."

"Then should we not share what is so plentiful? There are those who have never tasted such as these."

"Then load a team of pack animals, my friend, and tell them the Lhinian king withholds nothing from those who are in need."

"Even if the needy are Alingan?"

The audience was suddenly still. The king took only a moment to answer. His eyes shifted to Eghan's face. "Even so," he said.

Khalwyd took a huge bite of the apple and smiled around it.

Eghan leaned toward his father. "When can we leave, Father? May we take meat and potatoes as well? And clothing, and ..."

"What is this "we?" The king's frown made Eghan hold his breath. "You are not home an hour and you are wanting to leave again?"

Eghan heard the hurt in his father's voice. He answered more quietly. "They need the food and clothing badly, Father."

"Then it shall be taken to them. But you are heir to the Lhinian throne, Eghan, not a messenger boy."

Eghan remembered that tone in his father's voice and dropped his eyes. The look of disappointment on his face must have been apparent. The king put a hand on his shoulder. "But we can discuss all of that later."

Gherin leaned back and others questioned Eghan and his companions while the feast continued. Each one told parts of the adventure, Gherin asking questions now and then until the picture was complete. Then it was Eghan's turn to ask questions. He turned to his father.

"As we rode through the valley I noticed the people seem happier than I remember them. Or is it just that I have been so long among the Alinga?"

Gherin beamed. "What you have noticed is the result of much prayer, Eghan. The people are free now to study the Book, to worship and praise their God as they wish, if they wish. They know their king not only supports them, but is one of them."

Eghan smiled at the light in his father's eyes. It was the same fire he had seen first in his Uncle Adlair, and in Nara, and then in Khalwyd. Seeing it now in his father thrilled him most of all.

Gherin's face shone as he told how the people were responding to the Word of The One True God. "We are even building a special house - a house of prayer where the people can gather. I have hired the best stonemasons in the country, Eghan," he said with obvious pride. "It will be a house that will stand for generations."

"I look forward to seeing the construction of such a building," Eghan said.

The feast over, Khalwyd and Silhas excused themselves. The king rose and shook their hands again. "Rest well, both. Tomorrow we will talk about your reward." They bowed and left the hall.

Gherin turned to Eghan. "I am sure you must be weary too, Eghan. You may take your leave now, if you wish."

Eghan nodded, then stood and bowed to the king. "Thank you, Father, for the way you have received us this night."

"It is no more than your due," Gherin answered.

Eghan had only taken a few strides when his father was beside him again. "I will walk with you to your chambers," he said.

Eghan raised his eyebrows but did not object. When they reached the doors to his rooms, he noticed the sentry standing at attention close by. He was about to dismiss him when his father opened the doors, stepped into the room and pulled him into an embrace again. "I will see you in the morning."

Eghan pulled away from him, glancing at the large bed, where a thick quilt was turned down, several soft pillows arranged at its head.

"I am not certain I will be able to sleep on that. I have gotten used to pine boughs and a thin blanket on the ground."

Gherin laughed. "I think you will find this is much more to your liking. God keep you this night, son. The sentry will remain at your door."

"Thank you, again, Father, but surely that is not necessary."

"Perhaps not, but it will be so nonetheless."

When his father was gone, Eghan pulled off his tunic and sat in the middle of the bed. He spread his arms wide and flopped back onto the pillows. There were some things he was going to like about being home.

Chapter Two

Nara stared at her reflection in the long glass her handmaid held up. She grinned at her first thought: Eghan would not call me a stable-boy now. The young woman who looked back at her was dressed in a flowing blue gown sewn with jewels and trimmed in gold. Her black hair lay in a soft curve at her throat where her servant girl had just fastened a single pearl pendant. Nara grinned again, this time at the girl smiling at her from behind the mirror.

"What do you think, Brynna?"

"Oh, m'lady, I have never seen anyone so beautiful."

"Thanks to your skill with a needle and thread, my girl."

"No, m'lady. It is you that is beautiful, not just the dress."

Nara stepped forward and took the glass from her. "Well, enough of this vanity. I do thank you for all your work. I fear I would have been crowned in a tunic and trousers if it were not for you."

Brynna clapped a hand to her mouth and giggled.

A knock on the door sobered Nara as her handmaid rushed to answer it. She was back in a moment.

"It's Gage, m'lady."

"Show him into the outer room."

It did not take Nara long to change. In a few moments she was looking and feeling more like herself in a long tunic loosely belted. The tall man dropped to one knee before her. Nara extended her hand to him warmly and raised him up.

"General. It seems like weeks since I have seen you."

"Not so long as that, my lady, but it has been too long and I apologize. The work has kept me very busy."

"And I see it is going well. The market place is full of people and the new homes being built by your army look sturdy and are no doubt a great encouragement to the people."

Gage smiled and his eyes gleamed. "Yes. The people have never been so industrious, nor, I dare say, so happy. And it is not difficult to motivate them, with your coronation so close at hand."

Nara took a deep breath. "I just hope Burke is not planning too elaborate a ceremony. I prefer it to be quite short and to the point."

"But my lady, it has been a long time since we Alingans have had a queen to crown. You would not rob us of our pleasure, would you?"

"No, Gage, but I want the people to remember from whom their victory has come. The glory does not belong to me, but to The One True God."

"And He will be glorified, you may trust Burke and Adlair to see to that."

Nara nodded. "I know." She smiled up at him. "You will be on the platform, will you not?"

He nodded. "It will be my honor, to stand as witness."

"And as one who had a large hand in the defeat of our enemy. Some of the commendation should also go to you."

"I have been well rewarded, my lady. But ... there is one thing I wish you would allow me to see to."

Nara grinned. "Only one?"

"An important detail. I would like to order the construction of your residence...."

"I have a residence, Gage," Nara interrupted. "I am quite comfortable here."

"But my lady..."

Nara held up her hand. "We have discussed this before, my friend. Until the people throughout this kingdom are comfortably housed, fed and clothed, we will not spend time, energy nor resources on anything else."

"But my lady," Gage objected again. "Surely once you are crowned you should have a suitable castle in which to live."

"I do not need a castle, Gage. Perhaps in a few years, when things are more stable..."

"But it will take years to build. We should begin now."

"Years? I do not need an enormous house, Gage. There will be plenty of time to design and build one, some day. For now, we have more important things to attend to."

Gage gave a quick bow and took a step backwards. "As you wish, my lady."

Nara smiled. "How is your family?"

Gage's face brightened. "Very well, thank you. My wife takes chills easily, but otherwise she is completely recovered from her time in Malnar's dungeon."

"And your son?"

"He grows an inch a day, I swear it, and eats enough to prove himself my son."

Nara laughed. "That is good to hear."

Gage's face darkened a bit. "I do wish we had found conclusive evidence that Malnar's cohorts were killed when the castle fell. I would sleep easier at night."

"The kingdom was not restored so that it can be snatched away again, Gage. I believe the Lord will keep us all safe, whatever may happen."

The man nodded, looking sheepish. "Of course. But there is one other detail we should attend to..."

"Oh? Another one?"

Gage's words rushed out, as though he knew he was going to be interrupted again. "I would like to appoint a security guard that will constantly be with you, my queen. It need not be large, my lady, but..."

Nara held up her hand to silence him again. "Gage, you are a stubborn man."

Gage bowed. "Yes, my lady. I am."

Nara laughed. "How many times will you come to

me with the same request?"

The man's eyes were serious. "Until you say yes, my lady."

Nara paced to the window and stood with her back to him for a few moments. When she turned she nodded. "Very well. I will accept your advice in that matter. You may place two men to guard me, but they must keep their distance and respect my privacy. Agreed?"

"But perhaps four men would be..." He stopped when Nara held up her hand. "Very well. Two men. We are agreed. I will arrange it immediately. Now, if you will excuse me, I should get back to work. You are sure about the residence?"

Nara sighed. "Very sure."

Gage gave a quick grin. "Very well. I will not trouble you with it again, at least, not for a while."

Nara laughed. "Do not work too hard, my friend."

Gage bowed, turned on his heel and left the house.

Chapter Three

Eghan woke to a loud rapping on his door. He blinked in the bright sunlight, sat up and looked around. For a few moments he did not know where he was, then remembered and called out, "Enter."

Khalwyd strode into the room. "So, you are finally awake. A few days in your father's house and you have gotten lazy again."

Eghan stretched and flopped back on the pillows. "Have I missed breakfast?"

Khalwyd grunted. "And you will miss the mid-day meal as well, if you do not move."

"Then why did you not bring me something to eat?"

"You know where the kitchen is."

Eghan tightened his grip on the pillow behind his head, quickly raised himself and flung it at his guardian. Khalwyd threw it back and in one motion leaned forward and pulled the quilt from the bed.

Eghan leaped up, laughing. "All right, all right, I'm up." He pulled on the clothes laid out for him, then eyed his guardian and friend. His unruly red hair and beard had been trimmed and he was dressed in a fine dark green tunic.

"I see a few days in my father's house have changed you, as well, Khalwyd of Stohl."

The man smiled and stroked his chin. "Your father's barber does a fine job." He glanced down at himself. "His tailor does as well."

"And how do you sleep on your feather bed?"

"Like a baby." He laughed. "But I was up at dawn today."

"Doing what?"

"Attending to a business you might have enjoyed."

Eghan cocked his head and waited as the man strode to the window and motioned for him to look. They peered down at a string of mules laden with sacks and bundles. Servants were still lashing more to the small animals that already looked over-burdened. Eghan turned away, frowning.

Khalwyd peered at him. "I thought you would be pleased."

"That my father is as good as his word, yes, and that the Alingans will benefit."

"But?"

Eghan sighed and shrugged. "I wish I could go with them. Yet, I want to stay. I don't know, Khal. Being here, it all seems so different." He glanced out the window again. "I almost wish we were back in the caves."

Khalwyd laid a hand on his shoulder. "Give it time, Eghan. In a way, we are like returning soldiers, home from the war. It is normal that you will feel a bit displaced for a time."

"You feel it too?"

Khalwyd nodded. "A vague sense of restlessness and even loss."

"Yes, but there is something more. It is almost as though we are about to lose an important battle, but no-one cares, no-one is aware." Eghan stared out at the scene below. People barely glanced at the laden pack animals being slowly led toward the castle gates. "No-one senses any danger."

Khalwyd cocked his head. "You do?"

The boy shivered. "I cannot shake the uneasiness." He shrugged. "It may be just that everything has changed." He turned from the window and spoke softly. "I am not sure my place is here, anymore."

"The adjustment may not be easy, Eghan, but your place is here, as..."

"I know, I know ... as my father's only son and heir of the House of Lhin." He smiled. "And you had better get used to calling me Prince Eghan again, or my father may have something to say about it."

Khalwyd nodded. "He has been asking for you, Prince Eghan."

Eghan took a last look as the mules plodded through the gates. He whispered a quick prayer for their safe travel, turned and strode purposefully out of his room.

****

Gherin was in the main hall, hearing cases of complaint from various men. Some were noblemen with their entourage of courtiers, but others were common folk. Eghan was surprised to see them. It had not been the king's custom to hear the complaints of farmers and villagers. Eghan stood to the side, listening and watching as his father made decisions and dispensed justice, showing a wisdom and mercy Eghan admired.

When the court was dismissed, Gherin called him to his side. "Did you sleep well?"

Eghan grinned sheepishly. "Perhaps too well and too long, Father."

The king smiled, then quickly sobered. "That must change. It is time you began to follow a schedule, again, Eghan. Your studies have been long neglected. Silhas has set out a routine for you and a schedule for study of The Book as well. I think it would be best if you began tomorrow."

"Yes, Father."

Gherin raised his eyebrows. "No objections?"

"Not yet."

Gherin chuckled. "Khalwyd will carry on with your martial training as well. The rest of your time will be spent with me. I want you to join me every morning for prayer, and I want you by my side during these court sessions. It is important for the people to see you there and it is important that you learn how to administer the realm that will someday be yours."

"Praying with you will be an honor, Father. And I

can see I have much to learn about dispensing justice, especially to the common people. Your rulings today were very wise."

"The Lord has been teaching me the wisdom of mercy, Eghan, among other things, but I fear I am no Solomon. Judging and finding solutions to the problems of our people is one of the most difficult of my duties, but it is a good way to stay in touch with them."

"No doubt I will find it so, also," Eghan said softly.

The king clapped him on the back. "It also makes me hungry. Come. The table is set."

Eghan ate very little. Silhas chattered to him about the studies he had been preparing, but Eghan only half heard. The conversations floated around him but he remained detached. Finally he excused himself. Khalwyd half rose from his chair when he stood to leave, but Eghan saw the king place a hand on his arm as he said softly, "Let him go."

Eghan found himself in the stables. He wandered through them, watching boys currying the animals and cleaning stalls, men doctoring horses and mending saddlery. The king's stables were never quiet. It took him a while to find his horse. When he did, the animal was tethered outside a stall being cleaned by a ragged boy. Eghan watched for a while, until a clod of rotten straw was flung high, hitting him on the chest. The stable boy gasped when Eghan called out and wiped himself off.

Eghan smiled. "You do your work with enthusiasm."

The boy stared without answering.

"What is your name?"

"La ... Latham, m'Lord."

"Well, Latham, do you know what horse it is you have the privilege of tending?'

The boy shook his head. "I just cleans the stalls, m'Lord."

"Ah, yes. A stable boy is not allowed much else, is he?" Eghan remembered his resentment when his uncle had made him work in his stables yet refused to allow him to ride the fine horses. He stroked his horse's nose. "His name is Ezra. He was a gift from my uncle. Make sure you treat him well."

Latham nodded dumbly.

Eghan make his way into the saddlery room, where he selected a bridle and reached for a saddle. Before he could lift it, an older boy swept it up. "I'll do that for ye, Prince Eghan, no need to trouble."

Eghan took it from his hands. "No. I will do it myself." He felt the stares of the stable-hands as he carried the saddle to the stall. Ezra stomped the floor impatiently but Eghan did not hurry the grooming. He was enjoying the smells and sounds that had become familiar in a small stable hidden in the mountains.

By the time he bridled the horse and led it out into the air, its hide gleamed, its mane flowed like a feathered plume. Eghan swung into the saddle, laughing as Ezra pranced. He made the horse stand, then back up, then circle left and right before he was satisfied it would obey him. Latham was watching from the doorway, wide-eyed. Eghan nodded to him. "Clean the stall well, boy." He squeezed his knees together slightly and the horse leaped into a quick trot. Eghan guided him straight to the castle gate.

He was aware that more than a few heads turned as he rode through the marketplace and that more than a few of the heads were female. Eghan paid them no attention, but held Ezra to a slow trot until they were well away from the castle walls. He halted the horse on the crest of a low hill.

Below them stretched a long ribbon of grasses bending in a gentle breeze, sending a faint sweet smell to meet them. Ezra stamped. Eghan grinned as he felt the animal's tension mount, then clamped his thighs tightly around him and let the reins slip through his fingers. In a matter of seconds they were pounding over the ground, Ezra's neck stretched out, his ears flattened and nostrils flared. Eghan could barely breathe and his eyes filled with water as the wind cut at them, but he let the horse run.

Finally, his heart racing as wildly as the animal's, he began to pull back on the reins. When the horse thundered on without responding, Eghan had a moment of panic. He reached out and pulled with all his strength, shortening one rein, forcing Ezra to Turn. The horse's pace slowed and Eghan sat upright, once again in control, but his chest was still heaving by the time they slowed to a walk.

Eghan wiped the perspiration from his forehead with the sleeve of his tunic, leaned forward and patted the horse's damp neck. "I think we both needed that, Ezra, but do not expect me to let it happen again, anytime soon." He turned the horse back toward the castle.

As he rode he noted the fields were newly cut, the crops only recently taken in. He remembered the days in the high meadows when he helped the Hunstmen take in their hay crop. He remembered Nara's smile when they stopped to rest and breathe in the freshness of the day. He wondered if he would ever see her smile again.

Chapter Four

Eghan sat quietly in the large study next to his bedroom and waited for Silhas' tirade to finish. His tutor had been chiding him for daydreaming.
"If you were younger I would take a switch to you, prince or no prince. You must concentrate, Prince Eghan."

Eghan sighed and mumbled, "Forgive me, Silhas. But I know these stories and the history of my people well. Studying them again seems pointless."

"Pointless?"

Eghan raised his eyes at the pitch of Silhas' voice. His tutor's face went red with exasperation. "These "stories," as you call them are the legacy of your ancestors, Prince Eghan. It is important that ..."

He was interrupted by a knock and Eghan turned to see Khalwyd enter without waiting for permission. "He is mine, now, Silhas."

The advisor threw up his hands. "You can have him, he is certainly not listening to me!"

Khalwyd grinned but raised an eyebrow at Eghan as he stood and walked to the window. They were in one of the highest rooms of the castle, so he could see beyond the courtyard to the market square. It bustled with activity. Men called out from laden stalls as women strode by with full baskets on their hips. Hawkers moved among the crowd, holding up their wares, stopping anyone who slowed his pace. Here and there jugglers and acrobats performed for copper coins thrown at their feet. Eghan whirled around, pulling his tunic off as he strode into his bedroom. "I am going out, Khalwyd."

The guardian was on his heels. "Out? Out where?"

"Into the square, maybe beyond. It has been a long time since I have been among my own people."

"But it is time for ...."

"There is no need for you to go with me. I know my way around."

Khalwyd snorted. "If you think I am going to let you out of my sight, you are mistaken, my prince. The king was not happy that you rode out on your own yesterday."

Eghan pulled on his old Alingan shirt and grinned over his shoulder. "Very well, but keep your distance." He tossed him a worn Alingan cloak. "And put this on."

Servants bowed and curtsied but gave them quizzical looks as the two strode down the corridors and out of the castle. It was obvious the people outside, however, did not realize their prince was among them. Whenever he had been allowed beyond the courtyards of his father's house it was always in the company of a large entourage, always on horseback or in a carriage. Now in a ragged tunic, Eghan roamed on foot in the marketplace, enjoying the sounds and activity. He stopped at a stall selling fresh bread and picked up a dark loaf. "How much?" he asked the baker, who looked like he had indulged a bit too often in his own wares.

"Ah, you are a man of good taste, young man. What you have in your hand is my wife's prized molasses bread. There is none better, not even on King Gherin's table!"

Eghan grinned, delighted the man did not recognize him. "I will give you a pittance for it, then."

"A pittance? A pittance for the best bread in the valley?" The man snatched it from his hand. "Go home and bake your own for your pittance."

Eghan laughed. "How much, then?"

The baker looked him up and down, his eyes resting for a moment on Eghan's polished boots. "A piece of silver, and nothing less."

As Eghan made a mental note to complete his disguise next time, he whistled. "Silver! You prize your wife's cooking too highly, my friend. But," he nodded to Khalwyd who rolled his eyes and dug in his belt for the coin as Eghan finished, "I am hungry!" Khalwyd slapped it down on the stall and the baker snatched it up, his grin wide.

Khalwyd grunted. "It had better taste as good as you say it does."

Eghan turned away, chuckling as Khalwyd followed after him. He broke off a chunk and offered it to his guardian. "He is right, Khal, it is better than anything on my father's table." Before Khalwyd could answer, Eghan turned sharply toward the noise of banging hammers and sawing wood. They broke out of the market place and stood on the edge of a construction site. Stone masons were at work building walls, carpenters constructing scaffolding and framing for doors and windows. Eghan chewed his bread and watched the activity for a while, then approached one of the workmen.

"What are you building here?"

The man barely looked up. "The House of Prayer and worship, by order of King Gherin."

"The House of Prayer," Eghan repeated. He handed Khalwyd the bread. "Then let me help." He reached for a tool but the workman grasped his arm before he could pick it up.

"Are you skilled?"

"No, but I can work."

The man shook his head. "The king has ordered that only skilled craftsmen may work here, other than those who labor at mixing mortar and such."

Eghan straightened. "I am willing to do anything."

"Then speak to that man there, the one with no tunic. His name is Jharl."

Eghan turned to the one indicated. He was a huge man, his bare torso muscled and tanned. Eghan watched as he lifted a timber as though it were a splinter.

Khalwyd stepped to Eghan's side and hissed in his

ear. "This is no place for you, Eghan. You are the king's son!"

Eghan nodded. "And a King's house is being built. I want to have a hand in it." He strode forward boldly and called out to the laborer. Jharl turned at the sound of his name, but only gave Eghan a quick glance and returned to his work without responding.

Eghan went closer. "I want to work."

The man looked him over from head to toe and laughed. "Then go home and help your mother in her kitchen, boy. The work here is for men."

As the man turned away, Eghan caught his arm. "The Lord's work is for everyone who is willing."

Jharl's eyes rested on Eghan's boots for a moment, then he peered into his eyes. "You are willing to do a laborer's job?"

Eghan thought of the day his uncle had asked him a similar question. He nodded. "Even the work of a servant."

Jharl squinted. "Then take off those fine boots. You won't want to get them dirty." He turned away, then hesitated and confronted Eghan again. "Ye didn't steal them, did ye?"

Eghan shook his head as he pulled off the boots and handed them to Khalwyd. "No," he said, "I didn't steal them."

Jharl grunted. "Follow me, then."

Khalwyd started to protest again but before he could, Jharl addressed him. "What about you? Ye look like ye've got a day's work in ye."

Eghan was grinning. Khalwyd gave him a look but nodded. Jharl led them to a large mud hole. Several boys stood stomping in it up to their knees, while others threw in straw and coarse dirt. A few men mixed a thicker sludge at one end with wooden paddles and loaded the muck onto hand carts.

Jharl motioned at Eghan. "The paddles are over there." Then he jerked his chin at Khalwyd. "You can handle a cart."

The sun was setting when Jharl returned and called a halt to the work. Eghan dug his paddle into the ground and leaned on it, drawing his arm across his moist forehead. Khalwyd sank down beside him.

The foreman stood over them and dropped three coins into their hands. "I will expect ye both to be back tomorrow."

They answered at once. Eghan said "Yes." Khalwyd said "No."

Jharl looked from one to the other and grinned. The foreman assured them their hard work would be rewarded with something more satisfying if they returned the next day.

Eghan nodded. "We will be back."

As they trudged into the castle, Khalwyd groaned and rolled his shoulders. "The next time you invite me to stay home, remind me of today."

Eghan grinned and was about to answer when he was interrupted by his father's voice.

The king stared at them. "Where have you been?"

He took in their filthy appearance in one glance. "And what have you been doing?"

"Building the Lord's house." Eghan beamed.

The king's eyes flashed. "Khalwyd, you are responsible for ..."

"It was not Khal's fault, Father," Eghan interrupted. "I wanted to work."

"Work? Like a common laborer?"

"Very common," Khalwyd mumbled.

Eghan chuckled but quickly stifled it at the look on his father's face. The king was frowning. "Clean yourselves up and come to the dining hall. I want to talk to you both."

They bowed as Gherin whirled away. Eghan looked at Khalwyd. "I am afraid I have gotten you into trouble."

Khalwyd sighed. "You do seem to have a talent for it." He grinned. "But at least we won't be mixing mortar tomorrow."

"Do not be so sure."

Khalwyd stared. "He will not allow you to go wandering so freely among the people, Eghan."

As Eghan walked away, he hoped his determination came through in his voice. "It's Prince Eghan. And my place is among them."

They met the king in the dining hall. Eghan's mouth watered at the smell of the food, but he was not invited to sit down. The look on his father's face reminded him of days he had thought were long gone.

"I will not allow you to put yourself in danger,

Eghan. From now on you will stay within the castle walls unless you have my permission to go elsewhere."

"But ..."

"There is nothing to discuss. Khalwyd, you are to see to it."

Eghan bristled. "I want to know the people I will one day rule, Father. I must be among them to know them."

Gherin shook his head. "The danger is too great."

"Khalwyd will be with me."

"One man is not enough protection." He glanced at Khalwyd. "As we have seen in the past."

"I have more than one man. I lived among our enemies and was protected. Surely the Lord will protect me here as well, among my own people."

Gherin stared into Eghan's face, and for a moment he thought the king seemed to soften. Then his eyes clouded. "No, Eghan. I could not bear it if anything were to happen to you again. You will remain within the castle walls."

Eghan started to speak but his father held up his hand, then waved at the food-laden table. "Come now, you both must be hungry."

Eghan wheeled away. "Not any more."

"Eghan!"

He stopped but did not turn around.

"I will not tolerate disrespect. Come and sit at my side. Now."

Eghan clenched his hands into fists as he took a deep breath, turned and obeyed. They ate in silence.

Khalwyd seemed to be the only one with an appetite.

When the meal was over, Eghan stood and coolly addressed the king without facing him. "May I be excused, Father?"

Gherin did not answer until Eghan finally looked at him. Then he nodded. Eghan was half way to the doors when his father called his name again.

"I will pray about this, but until you hear differently you are to remain within the castle grounds. Understood?"

Eghan nodded. "Yes, Father."

Gherin watched him go, then turned to his son's guardian. "Keep him occupied, Khalwyd. It is boredom that makes him want to wander."

"Not just boredom, Sire. He genuinely wants to be with the people. He believes he belongs there."

"He belongs at my side."

Khalwyd leaned forward. "Perhaps the Lord wants him in both places, Sire. Is it too much to expect that the people would love their king and their prince enough to protect him?"

Gherin sat back, rubbing the long line of his jaw. Perhaps Khalwyd was right. And what did they have to fear, really, here in his own kingdom? He sighed. The memory of hearing that Eghan had been abducted was still raw. The agony of waiting to hear if his son was alive or dead had been almost too much for him to bear. *But we are safe, now,* he thought. *We are all safe and I know God has great things in store for the kingdom. Perhaps I am being too protective of my son.*

Chapter Five

The next morning Eghan and Khalwyd were summoned to prayer and breakfast with the king. Half way through the meal Eghan tossed his bread onto his plate. "There is a baker in the market who sells bread with twice the flavor of this."

His father seemed to attempt to hide a smile. "Indeed?"

Khalwyd snorted. "And charges a fortune for it."

"Perhaps if he thought he was selling to a peasant, the price would be more reasonable," Eghan hinted.

The king frowned. "And what if he learned that peasant dined at the king's table? Would he not have reason to feel cheated?"

Eghan peered at his father. "You once taught me that deception had its place."

"As a believer in The One True God, I now believe in truth." Gherin sighed as Eghan dropped his eyes. They continued to eat in silence but Eghan stole glances at his father, trying to gauge if his resolve was weakening.

When the king spoke again his voice was softer.

"Trusting Him must be balanced with reason and practicality, Eghan."

Eghan did not hesitate. "I have trusted him with my life for over a year, Father. He has never deserted me."

Gherin's smile was brief. "Perhaps, when you have a son of your own, you will understand how difficult it is for a father to trust anyone with his son's life, even the God he believes in."

Eghan leaned forward. "But we should, we must trust Him."

The king stood and paced for a time before returning to the table and responding. "Yes." He sighed. "We must." He turned to Khalwyd. "Leave his side and it will mean your death."

Eghan leaped up. "Thank you, Father."

Gherin smiled back. "Bring me some of that good bread, if it does not cost you the moon."

****

Jharl raised his eyebrows at the sight of them. "The boy won out, I see."

Khalwyd lifted his head a notch. "What do you have for us today? More mud?"

The foreman shook his head, turned and beckoned them to follow. "You will work with Ulhrik today. He is the most skilled of all our stone builders but his back is no longer strong enough to lift the heavy stones. You two will do it for him."

Khalwyd sighed and tilted his head at Eghan but he gave him only a grin in response. They followed Jharl to a half-built wall. An old man sat leaning against it, putting bits of dark bread into his mouth. When Jharl's shadow fell on him he looked up, grasped a gnarled walking stick and stretched out his hand, allowing the foreman to pull him to his feet.

"These are your workers today, Ulhrik."

The old man grinned, showing a line of toothless gums. "I hope they are better than the last two you sent me, Jharl." He waved his stick at Eghan. "That one does not look strong enough."

"He is not as scrawny as he looks. I watched him out-work grown men yesterday."

Ulhrik grunted. "Leave us to it, then."

Jharl nodded and walked away. The old man hobbled along the wall until it was only a single line of foundation stones. He motioned to a large pile of rock near-by and looked at Eghan. "Bring them, one at a time." He waved his hand at Khalwyd. "You, get us a cart load of mortar."

Khalwyd sighed loudly and stomped off.

Eghan looked at the pile of stones, selected one and stooped to pick it up. He grunted with its weight and mumbled, "One at a time. Does he think I could lift more?"

For the rest of the morning they worked, Eghan bringing the stones, placing them wherever Ulhrik pointed, helping the old man shift and grunt them into place. Khalwyd kept up a steady flow of mortar and helped lift the heavier stones.

Often Eghan thought he had placed a rock

perfectly, only to have Ulhrik order him to shift it one way or the other. Each time, Eghan felt it slip into place, wedged so tightly it could not be moved. The old man's eyes were keen. His hands never stopped moving over the stone.

Eghan did not argue when Khalwyd suggested they stop to take a breath after lifting a large boulder into place. They leaned on the wall and watched as Ulhrik examined it closely.

"How many walls have you built, old man?" Khalwyd asked.

"Too many to count, but I remember them all. None have been alike. None have been as important as these."

Khalwyd raised his eyebrows. Eghan too leaned forward to listen. "Why so?"

"These walls have waited generations to be built. I believe the Lord will keep them standing for generations to come, even as others fall, if the king and his son are faithful."

Eghan gave Khalwyd a quick glance before asking, "Faithful to what?"

"To their God, to their people. Fine, strong walls can be raised but if the kings are not faithful the walls will not serve them. The people will perish."

"A heavy responsibility for the king," Khalwyd commented.

"More so for the son," Ulhrik spoke over his shoulder. "The father has at last opened the doors. It will be for the son to step through them."

Eghan turned away and heaved a stone onto the wall.

Ulhrik shuffled over to him. "Not there, boy. Use your eyes. Here. Put it here," he said, tapping the wall with his stick.

Eghan moved the rock into place and shifted it until he felt it rest solidly. Ulhrik nodded. "Yes. You have good hands. Train the eyes and you may be good enough to apprentice some day." The old man cackled as though he had just told some outrageous joke.

Eghan stared, then could not help but grin at the mischief in the old eyes. He laughed aloud with him. *The son of Gherin Lhin, an apprentice stone builder. That is a good joke.* He sobered as he thought, *I wonder if my father would see the humor in it.*

Khalwyd shook his head at the two of them and mumbled something about bringing another cart of mortar. Ulhrik stopped him. "No more today. Scrape the cart clean."

Khalwyd did as he was told, surprised when the old man climbed onto it and pointed with his stick. "That way, and mind the holes."

The guardian glanced at Eghan, shrugged and heaved the cart forward. He followed Ulhrik's directions, swerving to avoid the pot-holes as they made their way through the crowd. Eghan trotted beside them, grinning as Ulhrik gave Khalwyd a tongue lashing every time the cart jarred him.

Journey Through Fire and Smoke

It was not long before Eghan realized they were heading directly toward his father's castle. When they reached it, Ulhrik waved with his stick and Khalwyd steered them to a high wall. As they approached it, Eghan was amazed to see that the new construction, the House of Prayer, joined the castle. He knew this was one of the oldest sections of his father's house. Why here, he wondered, why attach the house of prayer at all? Ulhrik heaved himself off the cart and hobbled toward a corner. Eghan watched as he slowly lowered himself to his knees and began digging in the dirt with his stick. He barely hesitated when Eghan knelt beside him and dug with his hands.

They unearthed about a foot before Ulhrik stopped and smiled. His hand moved over the surface of the stone for some time, then he grabbed Eghan's wrist and placed the boy's hand beside his. "There. You feel it?"

Eghan felt indentations and moved the tips of his fingers over the rough, cold surface. "It feels like an inscription."

Ulhrik showed his gums. "My father's name, and mine, and the words, "To the Glory of The One True God."

Eghan stared. "You built this wall?"

Ulhrik heaved himself to his feet and looked up. "Every stone of it, at my father's side." He looked down at Eghan. "Under the watchful eye of your grandfather."

Eghan did not try to hide his surprise as Ulhrik cackled. "I knew who you were the moment I laid eyes on you." He started to hobble away. "You are much like him."

"I am?" Eghan leaped up and followed.

Ulhrik nodded. "He had good hands, too." The old eyes twinkled. "But he was very impatient." He turned away again and Eghan danced in front of him. "He worked with you, on this wall?"

The old man waved his stick. "The house of prayer was begun long ago, though your father believes it was his idea." He cackled and strode away. Eghan dashed after him. "Tell me more."

"Tomorrow," Ulhrik said. "Come work tomorrow and I will tell you all I remember." He tottered away and disappeared in the crowd.

****

At dinner, Eghan tried to choose his words carefully. "We worked on the walls today, Father."

"Oh? No shoveling mud?"

Eghan grinned. "We worked with an old man named Ulhrik. He said I would make a good apprentice."

The king snorted. "And did you tell him you already are an apprentice?"

"I did not have to. He knew me."

Gherin's hand stopped half way to his mouth. His eyes darkened. "It is inevitable that you will be recognized, Eghan. From now on a guard will go with you."

Eghan ignored that. "He says he knew my grandfather. He says my grandfather worked on the walls with him."

Gherin leaned back and stared. "He is lying."

"I don't think so, Father. He is very old. He worked on the oldest section of this castle when he was a boy. He showed us an inscription on the foundation stone, bearing his name and his father's and the words 'to the Glory of The One True God'."

Gherin shook his head. "My grandfather would never have allowed such an inscription."

"It is there, Father. I felt it with my own hand."

The king's eyes narrowed. "What did you say this old man's name was?"

"He is called Ulhrik."

The king's frown deepened. "Bring him to me. I would like to hear what he has to say."

"I am going to work with him again tomorrow," Eghan said softly.

Gherin hesitated, then nodded slightly. "Bring him for the evening meal, then."

Eghan raised his head in surprise. "You are inviting a stonemason to dine with us?"

Gherin nodded. "If he is good enough to apprentice my son, he is good enough to eat at our table."

Eghan glanced at Khalwyd and smiled.

Chapter Six

Ulhrik stared. "Am I being summoned, then?"

Eghan shook his head. "No. You have been invited to dine, not summoned."

"Ah. Invited. An invitation I cannot refuse, no doubt."

"He just wants to hear what you have to say about my grandfather. He thinks you are lying."

"Ah," The old man said again. Pressing his back to the stone wall he slid down to the ground, pulled a rag from his cloak and mopped at his head.

Eghan watched until he could not contain his exasperation. "I am beginning to wonder if you are lying myself. You promised to tell me everything you remember, yet I have been here most of the day and you have barely told me a thing I did not already know."

Ulhrik peered up at him and chuckled. "The grandfather's impatience shows itself at last. I thought it was there, just below the surface. Though I must say, you control it much better than he did."

Eghan squatted before him. "Tell me. Or better, come to my father's table and tell us both."

The old man mopped his head one more time, then peered at him again, his eyes suddenly very serious. "Gherin Lhin will not be happy to hear what I have to say to him. Nor will you."

Eghan tried not to show the sudden dread he felt. "What do you mean?"

Ulhrik cocked a thumb over his shoulder. "We must build these walls strong. They may be the only walls left standing."

Eghan frowned and leaned forward. "Explain yourself."

He tucked the rag back into his clothing and struggled to his feet, leaning heavily on Eghan's shoulder as they stood. When he was erect he stared toward the castle. "At your father's table, boy. At King Gherin's command."

****

The servants bowed and curtsied as the three approached, then stared at the ragged old man between Eghan and his guardian. The three made their way toward the dining hall, Ulhrik stopping to stare and exclaim now and then at the fine furnishings and tapestries. Once, he made them wait while he sat for several moments on a padded bench. Eghan rolled his eyes and sighed a great deal, but did not voice his impatience. When Ulhrik finally stood he cackled loudly, then picked up his walking stick and strode with a strong pace down the corridor. Eghan and Khalwyd exchanged amazed looks, then scurried to catch up with him.

When they arrived at the great hall, the old man did not wait to be announced, but thumped the doors loudly with his stick. Eghan was about to caution him when the doors swung open and Ulhrik strode forward.

The king and Silhas both rose from the table as the old man approached. Just when Eghan was sure his father would respond in anger to Ulhrik's lack of respect, the old man dropped to one knee and bowed his head. Gherin stepped toward him and raised him up, obviously amazed as he peered into his face. "You," he said.

Ulhrik smiled. His voice did not seem so old as he bowed his head slightly and responded with, "Your Majesty."

Silhas was frowning. "I thought you were dead, long ago."

"An assumption that was, obviously, incorrect."

"So you have been among us all this time?" the king asked. "Why did you not show yourself again, when I declared my belief? You must have known you would not be harmed?"

"There was no need."

"And now?"

"Now I must tell you, once again, I have had a vision."

Gherin's eyes clouded. "Tell me," he said.

Ulhrik glanced at the food-laden table. "I would eat and drink first."

Eghan was astonished when his father nodded and Silhas took the man's elbow to lead him to the table. Eghan threw a questioning glance at Khalwyd who shrugged in reply. They sat at the table and ate as the food was served but Eghan barely tasted it. He was fascinated at the obvious tension between his father and Ulhrik. As they talked of the past it was as though they were playing a game of chess. The old man was a master at telling a tale yet withholding information. Eghan wondered how long his father's patience would last. He was surprised to see him smile suddenly and raise his goblet.

Ulhrik cackled and raised his cup in return. "The king's table is as well supplied as I remember it, Your Majesty."

"You were a young man then, and I, much younger than my son."

Ulhrik nodded. "I remember you. Do you remember the prophecy?"

Gherin took a deep breath. "How could I forget something that foretold the destruction of The House of Lhin?"

"Your father chose not to remember."

"And to banish you from this kingdom."

The old man smiled. "My travels took me to many far away places. I have led a rather interesting life, thanks to your father."

"Your prophecy did not come true."

"We are still alive, you and I."

Gherin leaned forward. "Are you saying your vision still holds?"

"I am."

The king leaned back and studied him. "And you have had another?"

"Yes."

"Then speak it, man. We have had enough games between us."

Ulhrik turned slowly and looked at Eghan. "It came to me a few days before your son. In it, I saw him standing in the doorway of the House of Prayer now being completed. He had the sword of Lhin in his hand and all around him was fire and smoke."

For a long moment no-one spoke. Then Eghan leaned forward. "What did the first prophecy say?"

The king stood and paced, but said nothing other than orders dismissing the servants. He wandered to the hearth, staring at the small pile of cinders. Silhas, Khalwyd and Ulhrik remained seated at the long table. Finally, it was Silhas who answered.

"The prophesy was said to be a judgment on the people for turning away from God. The king, your grandfather, was enraged when Ulhrik burst into the hall, much like he did today, and spoke before being invited. I remember trembling, even as a child, at his words."

Khalwyd was frowning. "But surely, now, the prophecy is nullified. The people are turning back. More come to accept every day."

Ulhrik shook his head. "I wish it were so, but the consequences of sin live on. I believe the revival of faith is happening to prepare the people for what is to come."

Eghan watched his father slowly return and sit at the table. When the king did not speak, Eghan leaned forward again. "But what did the prophesy say, exactly?"

Ulhrik spread his boney hands in front of them. "The Valley of Lhin will be laid waste, the people will be scattered."

Eghan's pulse throbbed in his head. "Where will the enemy come from?"

"It will have a subtle beginning, but evil will invade and, for a time, will conquer. Only a remnant of the righteous will remain, and that, surrounded by evil."

Eghan watched the old man's face. "And you believe I will be the one to lead that remnant?"

Ulhrik nodded. "In time, yes."

"How much time?" Khalwyd asked.

"The Lord has not revealed that to me."

They sat in silence until the king stood. "We will not speak to the people of the prophesy yet. But we must prepare them for the days ahead."

Khalwyd's comment was almost to himself. "What could be done to prepare them for their own destruction?"

The king's voice was calm. Eghan was amazed at the strength in it. "We are all moving toward death, Khalwyd. The journey is made bearable, indeed joyful, only when we know the One who directs it."

Silhas nodded. "We must be diligent in spreading His truth."

"And the House of Prayer must be completed quickly," the king added.

Ulhrik stood. "I have worked on the drawings for this house for many years. It will be important that you and your son know every detail of its design."

Gherin gave him a rueful smile. "So, my son will be your apprentice, after all."

Eghan stared at his father, but could not bring himself to smile.

Chapter Seven

Nara placed a hand on a donkey's neck and watched as the bundles were unloaded. Already people had heard of the caravan and were swarming to the square, hoping for a share in the wealth. She looked up at the man beside her.

"The Lhinian king has shown a generosity I did not expect."

Adlair smiled. "Perhaps it was not so much the king's doing."

Nara dropped her eyes for a moment, then raised them again. "With this gesture of good will, we know his offer to trade was made in good faith."

Adlair nodded. "My brother-in-law is a practical man. I am sure our terms will meet with his approval when I tell him of the quality of the ore in your Alingan mines."

"When will you leave, then, Master Adlair?" She had turned to face him, knowing the sorrow in her eyes was plain.

"Immediately after your coronation."

She slipped into his arms then, and fought the tears. "Then I will be alone."

The tall man pushed her away gently. "A child of The One True God is never alone, Nara, and Gage and Burke..."

"Are faithful and true," she finished the sentence for him. "I know." She smiled briefly. "And I am a queen, not a child anymore. Forgive me, Master Adlair, but sometimes I wish for that childhood."

"Remember the words of the prophet Jeremiah written in the twenty-ninth chapter of his book, verse 11 -- "For I know the plans I have for you," declares the Lord, "plans to prosper you and not to harm you, plans to give you hope and a future." Hold on to that, Nara. It will be hard for awhile, but I believe the Lord will bless you beyond your heart's imagining."

Her face was glowing now. "He already has, Adlair. To see my people free again, and to be their queen, it has blessed me more than I could ever have believed possible."

They watched as the unloading progressed and Gage organized the people into groups to receive the food and clothing. Nara's handmaid approached with a deep green tunic over her arms. She held it out to Nara, smiling.

Nara shook her head. "You take it, Brynna."

The girl ran her hand over the fine cloth. "It is fit for a queen." She nodded at Nara's worn clothing. "And you need one."

Nara glanced down at herself and nodded. "I

suppose you are right." She held the garment up to herself and smiled as Brynna clapped her hands. She handed it back to her. "Be sure to find one for yourself, now. One fit for a queen's handmaid."

Brynna's eyes widened. She curtsied clumsily and whirled away.

Adlair chuckled. "There, you see? Again, He supplies your needs."

Nara laughed. "Yes. He always does." She rested her hand on his arm. "There are so many changes ahead, so much to do. I will miss you terribly, Master Adlair."

He put his arm around her. "What message would you like me to take to Eghan?"

She stepped back and dropped her head. "Tell him I am well and ..." she turned away and dropped her voice. "Tell him I miss him."

Adlair reached out and touched her chin, turning her head back toward him. When she raised her eyes to his, he spoke. "Perhaps there will be a day when you may tell him what is in your heart."

Nara sighed, then tossed her long dark hair over her shoulder. "How can that day ever be? He will be king of his people some day, and I am about to be crowned queen of the Alinga. We have two separate destinies."

"Yet the Lord may give you the desire of your heart."

Nara sighed again. "Or change my heart's desire."

Chapter Eight

Khalwyd stood with one hand on his hip, the other gripping the hilt of his sword. Its tip rested in the middle of Eghan's chest, pressing him against the wall. As Khalwyd stepped back he shook his head. "Too many mistakes, Eghan. You know better. You are not concentrating."

Eghan pulled a pair of thin leather gauntlets off his hands and ran his fingers through his hair. "My heart is not in it today, Khal."

"Then where, pray tell, is your heart?"

The look Eghan gave him made him frown. The prince shrugged and turned away. Khalwyd watched him go and made a mental note to speak to his father. Perhaps the king's plan was a good one after all, though Khalwyd still had a vague uneasiness about it. Gherin had told him a neighboring lord and his niece had been invited to visit the court. The king had been hearing reports of the girl's beauty and noble character. He was hoping his son would notice. A match would seal an alliance that Gherin said had been too long in the negotiating. They would be arriving any day but

Eghan had not yet been told. Khalwyd sighed. He suspected the prince would not take the news well. He sheathed his sword and called after him.

As Eghan turned, Khalwyd caught up. "There is a hunting party going out first thing in the morning. Perhaps we should join them."

"Ulhrik will be expecting us." Eghan's voice was tight.

"I am sure he can get along without us for one day. We both need a change of activity."

Eghan seemed about to agree, then changed his mind. He gave his head a hard shake and strode away. "We must continue the work."

Khalwyd kept pace with him. "Everyone needs a diversion now and then. I will tell the old slave driver we are going hunting."

Eghan gave him a quick grin. "Which one do you mean, Ulhrik or my father?"

Khalwyd snorted. "They have both been pushing you lately, haven't they?"

"It is understandable."

"But perhaps unnecessary."

Eghan stopped walking and faced him. "You doubt the prophesy?"

Khalwyd shook his head. "It is not that I do not believe it, but it seems everyone is too caught up in it."

"There is good reason."

"Yet if the prophesy is God's will, should we not be at peace? As your father said, we are all dying, yet we do not dwell morbidly on that fact. We live our lives as we think He wants us to, with joy, not dread. And besides, it could be many years before the prophesy will unfold."

Eghan turned away, then stopped and whirled back. "You are right. Absolutely right. He is in control, so what is there to fear?"

Khalwyd smiled at the sudden brightness on Eghan's face. "Right, so hunt with me tomorrow."

Eghan still hesitated, then nodded. "It has been a while since I gave Ezra a good run. Very well, Khal, I will join you."

Khalwyd slapped the boy's back. "Good. I will wake you just before dawn."

Eghan groaned. "So early?"

"There is nothing like the sight of the valley as the sun comes up. You will love it."

"If my eyes are open enough to see it."

"Oh, they will be open." Khalwyd laughed. "I guarantee it."

The next morning Eghan woke to feel two large hands grabbing his ankles. Before he could react he found himself on the cold stone floor, which made him leap to his feet. Khalwyd's laughter did not lighten his mood.

"Do you have to wake me like a rampaging bear?" Eghan let his voice show more than an edge of irritation.

Khalwyd chuckled again. "I tried the gentle approach but you kept on snoring. Get dressed or you will not get anything to eat before we leave."

Eghan ran a hand through his hair. "This had better be worth it," he mumbled.

The hunting party was quiet as they ate. Eghan studied the men. They were some of the most trusted of his father's household, brave, strong men who would die for their king and their prince, if need be.

God, may the need never arise, Eghan prayed. May they have only to hunt in the hills and then go home to their wives and children. Even as he prayed, Eghan knew there would be need, some day. He hoped it would not be soon.

When they finished their meal and moved to the courtyard where the horses waited, Eghan looked for Ezra. Latham, the young boy he had met in the stables, stood holding the horse's reins. Eghan smiled. The lad looked like he was asleep on his feet. Eghan slipped up behind him and yanked the reins out of his hand. The boy jumped, causing Ezra to toss his head and side-step. Grabbing the horse's bridle, Eghan chuckled. "They got you out of bed too early, did they, Latham?"

The lad's eyes were round. "I am so sorry, m'lord. It will not happen again, sir, I swear."

Eghan put a hand on his shoulder. "It's all right. I have trouble getting out of bed so early myself."

Latham grinned. "It was a bit earlier than usual, sir."

"Well, you can go back to sleep when we are gone."

"Oh no, m'Lord. I would get a thrashin' if I was to do that, sir."

Eghan mounted and looked down at the boy. "Then your father is too harsh with you."

"Me father's dead, sir."

Ezra had started to prance with impatience and Eghan barely heard the boy's soft voice. Forcing his horse to stand, he turned back to reply but saw Latham dart out of the way as the company started to move out.

Guiding Ezra in a circle, he spotted him again, watching from the safety of a doorway. Something about the boy tugged at him. He nudged his horse closer. "Be here when we get back," he called out. "I want you to take care of Ezra."

Latham's face shone. "Yes, m'lord. Oh my, yes. I will be here, m'lord."

Eghan tossed him a grin as the group formed into twos and trotted out of the courtyard.

Khalwyd was right. The valley was beautiful as the sun rose above it. Eghan watched as the light grew from faint beams to broad shafts striking the orchards and fields, making them glow. He found himself praying again as he rode, praising God for this prosperous valley, a home that was beautiful and safe. He thanked God for what He had given them all and for a day to hunt. They rode into the low hills just as the sun was creeping up the slopes. Dismounting in a grove of trees, the men armed themselves without speaking. Khalwyd handed Eghan a bow and full quiver. They moved off quietly, spaced apart but within sight of each other. It was not long before a flock of birds was raised and several bagged. Eghan downed his share and received approving nods from some of the men.

They hunted until the sun began to warm their backs. Returning to the grove where the horses grazed, Khalwyd came along-side Eghan and laid a hand on his shoulder. "A good hunt."

"Yes. The cooks should be happy with such fine birds to stuff."

"The men say there is a stag in these woods that has been eluding them for months. Perhaps we should plan a longer hunt and see if we can bag him."

"I would like that, Khal, but..."

"The building." Khalwyd sighed. "Yes. Well, we can think about it."

Eghan thought about it as they headed back to the castle. He loved being out in the countryside again. He longed to wake to the smell of the earth beneath him and go to bed staring at the stars. He wanted to hunt again with Khalwyd, but could they spare the time? Was there time for leisure when the House of Prayer was still only half built? He wished he knew.

As they neared the castle, Eghan grew restless and Ezra sensed it, tossing his head. Eghan held him

back until Khalwyd was beside him. "I want to let
Ezra run. I will meet you before the evening meal."
Not waiting for Khalwyd's objection, he pressed one
leg hard into the horse's side and slid the reins high
on his neck. Ezra whirled away and leaped eagerly
into a full gallop.

Eghan was well away from the hunt party when
he glanced back and saw Khalwyd following at a
distance. Eghan knew his guardian had no chance
of catching him, but he also knew that he would not
leave him entirely alone. He let Ezra run a while
longer, then reined him in and entered a long
orchard at a slow canter, then let the horse wander
at a walk. When they came to a small creek Eghan
dismounted while Ezra grazed. He stretched out in
the lush grass and dozed until he heard Khalwyd's
horse approaching at a fast trot. He sat up just as he
became aware of the sound of more horses. His
heartbeat quickened and he leaped to his feet.

A large entourage was heading toward them, a
shining black coach sending billows of dust into the
air as it approached along the narrow road. The
coach was surrounded by well-armed horsemen. As
it drew closer Khalwyd leaped from his mount and
stood by Eghan's side, his hand on his sword.

Eghan sensed his tension. "What is it?"

Before Khalwyd could answer, the entourage
stopped and one of the horsemen bellowed.

"You there. How much farther to the castle of
Gherin Lhin?"

Khalwyd's eyes narrowed. "Two hour's ride."

The soldier sat back in his saddle and waved the group on without acknowledging Khalwyd's reply.

Eghan and his guardian turned away from the dust as the coach clattered by. Eghan frowned. "Who do you suppose that was?"

"Lord Rian Gille and his niece, the Duchess Malora."

Eghan stared at him. "You knew they were coming?"

"Your father told me a few days ago."

"Why was I not told?"

"He wanted to find the right time to speak to you about it himself. They have arrived more quickly than he anticipated."

"What was there to speak about that required the right time?"

Khalwyd looked away and did not answer. Eghan stepped in front of him. "Khalwyd?"

His guardian sighed. "Your father is hoping you will court the young woman," he blurted. "He feels it is time you took a wife and an alliance with their realm would be politically expedient."

Eghan's eyebrows shot up but he said nothing.

Khalwyd gave him a lopsided grin. "They say she is a beauty."

Eghan stared at him for a moment longer, then whirled away. "Then let her show it off in my father's court. I have no wish to see her. He grabbed Ezra's dangling reins and leaped into the saddle.

"Eghan, where are you going?"

Eghan had already turned his horse's head and had to reply by calling over his shoulder. "Perhaps I will track that stag for a few days." He pressed his knees together and let Ezra run. He ignored Khalwyd's call but glanced back to see him leap on his horse and charge after him. He spurred Ezra on.

It was almost nightfall when Khalwyd finally caught up. Eghan had lit a small fire and was preparing a bed of pine bows.

Khalwyd approached quietly. "Eghan, we must return to the castle at once. Your father will..."

"Leave me!" Eghan saw him clench his fists and stiffen, but before he could respond, Eghan sighed and apologized.

"I am sorry, Khal. I did not mean to speak that way, but I am not going home."

"You are being childish."

Eghan tossed a stick into the fire. "Perhaps because my father insists on treating me like a child."

"He has your well-being at heart, Eghan, as well as the kingdom's safety. You know that."

Eghan did not reply. Khalwyd's voice sounded more conciliatory when he said, "It is not as though a wedding has been arranged. Yet."

Eghan turned away and sat down on a log near the fire. Khalwyd moved closer and squatted. The two stared into the flames for some time. Then Khalwyd stood, took a knife from his belt and walked up the hillside, into the woods. When he returned with more pine bows, Eghan grinned.

Khalwyd threw the boughs down. "One night. Agreed?"

Eghan poked at the fire but nodded. "Agreed."

Khalwyd unsaddled his horse and removed a rolled blanket from it, took some bread and a water skin from the side bag and returned to the fire. They ate their meager supper in silence and stretched out on their beds as darkness descended around them.

Eghan stared at the stars, his mind flooding with memories until Khalwyd's voice broke his reverie.

"He is going to be furious."

"I know."

"We can still go back."

Eghan put his arms behind his head. "Not tonight, Khal. If I am to endure my father's manipulations, let me have this one night."

Khalwyd rolled over onto his back and Eghan heard him let out a deep breath. "It is good to be out. I have missed this."

Eghan was quiet for a while, then rolled onto his side and asked, "Do you ever wish you were not in the position you hold, Khal? Do you ever wish for a different life?"

The guardian shifted on his bed. "There have been times, like a few hours ago."

Eghan heard rather than saw the grin in Khalwyd's voice as he spoke into the darkness. "Seriously."

It took Khalwyd a while to respond. "Truthfully, yes, I have wished for more of a life of my own at times, but I gave a vow of loyalty to your father and to your family long ago, when I was not much older than you. I would rather die than break it."

"Honor and duty."

"Yes, honor, duty, but also, love." Eghan heard him roll towards him and watched the glow of the coals light his face. "Love can grow, Eghan," he said. "Even when our affections and desires have previously been, uh ... elsewhere."

Eghan rolled onto his back and sighed. It was a common thing for a father to choose a wife for his son, especially to forge a strong alliance with a neighbor. Eghan knew he should not have been surprised that his father had arranged this meeting, but he chafed at the fact that he had not even been told she was coming. Surely he deserved that courtesy. He was almost asleep when Khalwyd ventured a last comment.

"You may like her."

Eghan rolled away from him and pretended he had not heard.

Chapter Nine

The sun was rising when Eghan felt Khalwyd's boot nudge his backside. He rolled out of his blanket, stretched and blinked in the early light.

Khalwyd picked up their blankets. "If we are fortunate, your father will not have missed us yet."

Eghan snorted.

Khalwyd sighed. "Well, we can hope."

Their horses clattered into the courtyard just before the morning meal. As Eghan dismounted, Latham scurried toward him, rubbing at his eyes. The lad tried not to yawn as he took Ezra's reins. Eghan stared at him. "Have you been here all night?"

"Yes, m'lord, as you said, sir, I waited for ye."

"Where did you sleep?"

"There, sir."

When Latham pointed to the stone steps, Eghan groaned. "Forgive me, lad," he said. "I did not expect to be gone so long."

Latham's jaw dropped open and he stared. When he found his voice, he stammered. "N..n..no harm done, m'lord."

Eghan smiled at him. "Tend to Ezra. Then come and find me."

"M..my, oh, y..yes, m'lord."

They met Silhas as they entered the castle. The adviser looked relieved. "Thank the Lord. He was about to send troops out to search for you."

"Where is he, Silhas?"

"In the great hall, about to have breakfast with ... his guests."

Eghan glanced at Khalwyd. "We might as well get it over with."

As they strode down the corridor, Silhas called after them. "It might be advisable to clean yourselves up a bit first."

Eghan paused, glanced down at himself, then continued on, giving Khalwyd a quick grin.

Khalwyd strode after him. "Eghan, we must change."

"Why? I have no desire to make a good impression." He hurried forward.

"Eghan!"

"Change if you want to, Khal, I am going in as I am."

In the fleeting first moments when Eghan entered the hall he saw an expression on his father's face that he had never seen before. It was sad but soft, almost adoring as the king stared at the young woman seated at the long table, her back to Eghan and Khalwyd. Eghan stared as his father rose to greet him, aware of the whispering of the servants at the door. He rushed to speak before his father could reproach him. "I am sorry if you were worried, Father, but as you see, Khal and I are fine."

Gherin's face showed his displeasure as he took in his son's appearance, but he waved his hand. "We will talk later, Eghan. We have guests." He stepped forward and took the hand of the young woman seated near him. She had not turned when he spoke, so Eghan was not prepared for the loveliness of the young face that now smiled up at him. Suddenly he was ashamed of himself.

"Prince Eghan Lhin, I present Duchess Malora and her uncle, Lord Rian Gille."

Eghan bowed as they rose. Lord Rian looked down his long nose, his eyes moving over Eghan from his muddy boots to his disheveled head. "Does the prince often appear this way in his father's presence?"

Eghan frowned but spoke apologetically. "Forgive my appearance, Lord Rian, Duchess." He brushed a dried leaf from his tunic. "We have been hunting."

Malora took a small step forward and gave her uncle a quick look. "I am afraid my uncle knows little about hunting, Prince Eghan." Turning back to him, her face shone. "Were you successful?"

Eghan nodded and tried not to stammer. "Yes. We bagged a good number of birds. No doubt you will be sampling some of them in the days ahead."

"Then I am thankful." As she gave a smile and a small curtsy, Eghan realized he was staring.

He collected himself quickly. "If you will excuse me..."

"Yes, we will," the king replied. "I will be along shortly."

Eghan dropped his eyes at the tone of his father's voice, then bowed and left the hall, Khalwyd at his heels.

He had bathed and was rubbing his head dry in his chamber when he heard a light tapping on his door. When he responded, it opened a crack and a small head appeared. "It's me, Latham, m'lord."

Eghan smiled. "Come in, boy, come in."

"I'd've got here sooner, sir, but they kept chasin' me out before I could find ye. It took some schemin' to get in here."

"Something you are quite good at, I suspect." The boy blushed and Eghan chuckled. "Is Ezra settled?"

"Yes, m'lord. Comfortably, sir."

"Good." Eghan pulled a long tassel hanging down the wall as he eyed the boy. "How old are you, Latham?"

"Old, sir?" The boy cocked his head comically. "I don't know for certain, m'lord."

"A guess, then."

"Ten, eleven, twelve. What age would ye want me to be, sir?"

Eghan laughed again. "Any of those would be fine. Do you have any family?"

Latham shook his head. "None I knows of. I had a dog, but it died."

"I am sorry."

Latham shrugged. "That's the way 'o things."

Eghan watched him intently. "Do you like your work in the stables?"

The boy shrugged again and ducked his head. "Mostly."

"But?"

Latham studied him for a moment, then seemed to make a decision. "The older lads don't treat me real good, sometimes."

"Oh?"

He was quiet again, then spoke slowly, as though at each word he might stop. "They blames things on me, so's – so's I gets the thrashin's, when the work's not done."

"I see." The master of the wardrobe knocked and entered. Eghan waved toward Latham. "Give him a bath, new clothes and a bed in my chambers. And cut his hair. From now on, he is my personal page." Eghan grinned at the wide-eyed lad. "That is, if he wants to be."

"My, oh my, yes. Yes, m'lord, I do."

The servant looked distastefully at the boy and blinked. "But, my lord, the Chamberlain will not ... "

Eghan held up his hand. "I choose to have this boy as my personal servant. If the Chamberlain objects he can speak to me directly."

The servant bowed, tapped Latham's shoulder and led him away. Eghan was still grinning when his father arrived. The grin quickly faded.

"Do you realize how worried I was and how badly you embarrassed me before our guests?"

"I am sorry Father, but I was in no danger and Khal was with me."

"He tells me you deliberately stayed out because you were upset about the arrival of Lord Rian and the Duchess."

"You should have consulted me before inviting them."

"Consulted you?" The king's face was reddening. "Is this not my own house? Do I need my son's permission to invite a nobleman to my own court?"

"Only when you are scheming to have your son court that nobleman's niece."

"Many are betrothed in childhood without their knowledge nor consent."

"Times are changing, Father. I wish to decide when I will court, and whom I will court."

Gherin's anger flashed in his eyes. "You will obey me as long as you live in my house."

Eghan opened his mouth to answer, then thought better of it. He took a deep breath. "I mean you no disrespect, Father, but I am a man now. A man should be allowed to choose a wife for himself."

"You are a prince of the House of Lhin and heir to the throne, not some village peasant. You have a duty to that heritage, Eghan, and it is long past time you accepted it and lived up to it."

Eghan dropped his eyes. He heard his father sigh and looked up again, surprised to see the king's anger seep away. "I was younger than you when your mother was brought here. Our love grew from that day."

Eghan did not know what to say. It was the first time his father had ever mentioned his relationship with his mother. There was silence for a while, then Eghan turned to peer out the window. "How long will they be here?"

"A few months, perhaps the winter."

Eghan gave a curt nod. "I will spend some time with her, if it will please you, but I must make any further decisions myself."

Gherin sighed again, but nodded. "We will discuss it further at another time, then." He turned to leave, then hesitated. "She is lovely."

Eghan could not help but admit it. "She is," he said.

That night at dinner Eghan thought she was perhaps the most beautiful woman he had ever seen. She was dressed in a flowing gown of rich green silk, her golden hair pulled up at the back and falling softly over her shoulders in long ringlets. When she turned her blue eyes on him, he had to remember to breathe.

"Do you hunt often, Prince Eghan?"

"Not as often as I would wish. My time has been taken up with building, this past while."

"Building? Building what?"

"A house of prayer."

"Really? How intriguing. And what gods will you pray to when it is complete?"

"To The One True God, Duchess."

Malora laughed. "Surely you cannot believe there is only one god."

Eghan's stomach churned. He wanted to say yes, to tell her about his faith, but something in her eyes made him stop.

"It is important work," he fumbled.

She leaned toward him, placed her hand on his, and her eyes were suddenly soft again. "To be sure. Will you show me the building? Tomorrow perhaps?"

Eghan nodded and relaxed again, enjoying the feel of her hand on his. "If you wish."

As the meal continued Eghan noticed how his father treated the young woman with a deference he had never seen the king show anyone before. Gherin leaned toward her often, his eyes rarely leaving her face. He is totally mesmerized, Eghan thought, and I understand why. Such beauty could make fools of us all.

Chapter Ten

Ulhrik squinted as he saw them come. Prince Eghan was leading a young woman across the rough ground as though she were breakable. Ulhrik hobbled forward a few paces, then stopped. He could see her face clearly now, the flashing smile, the coy looks she tossed at the prince. Ulhrik grunted, whirled around and made his way beyond the wall to the enclosed room where the drawings and plans for the building were laid out. He moved as quickly as he could, rolling up the large papers and hiding them behind the door. Only one drawing remained when the two young people entered.

Eghan introduced them. "Ulhrik, this is the Duchess Malora, a guest in my father's house."

Ulhrik gave the girl an icy stare, not caring that the prince obviously noticed his lack of courtesy. Eghan turned quickly to her.

"M'lady, this is Ulhrik, the finest stone builder in the country."

Malora gave him a quick nod while waving a scented handkerchief in front of her face, but Ulhrik noticed her eyes were on the drawings on the table.

"Is this your plan for the building?"

Ulhrik did not answer. Eghan peered at him and the old man felt the boy's anger but he stared back and remained still and silent.

The prince stepped toward the table. "Yes...one of them." He shifted the paper and opened his mouth as he raised his head and looked at Ulhrik. He knew the prince was about to ask where the other drawings were. He gave his head a quick shake and hoped the look in his eyes was enough of a signal.

Eghan turned back to Malora, who was watching him intently. "The others are not yet complete," he said.

Ulhrik almost smiled. It was not a lie, but he knew the half truth would make Eghan feel uneasy.

Malora stepped forward and peered at the paper. "I can see it will be a fine edifice. Will it have no other purpose than prayer?"

"It will be a sanctuary." Ulhrik made his voice boom. They both stared. "And a house of prayer for those who wish to worship The One True God."

Malora smiled. "I see."

Ulhrik's tension increased as her lips twisted and her tone mocked him.

"And will you be one of the high priests, old man?" She laughed before either of them could respond. "No. I think not." She glanced again at the drawings, turned on her heel and stepped outside.

Eghan gave Ulhrik another glare, then followed.

Ulhrik remained just inside the door, hidden from their sight, but able to watch them and hear their voices.

"I apologize for his rudeness, Duchess."

"If I were at home, I would have him flogged."

Even from the doorway Ulhrik could hear the ice in the girl's voice and see her eyes flash. Then they changed so swiftly he wondered if he had mistaken the look. She smiled at the prince. "Workers can be difficult, can they not? But if they do their work ..."

Eghan nodded. "He is very skilled. We could not build this house as we have planned, without him."

"Why does it take such skill? It looks to be very ordinary."

Ulhrik held his breath. Be wise, boy, he thought. Be wise.

Eghan was staring into her eyes and for a moment Ulhrik thought he was going to tell her everything, about the prophesy, the plans being made to prepare for it, the plans to ensure that this building would indeed be a refuge. Ulhrik considered bursting out before the boy had the chance to speak. But then Eghan shrugged.

"Even an ordinary house takes skill when it is built to stand for generations." He looked away as he took her arm and guided her toward the carriage. As he helped her climb into it, she turned back to him. "You are not coming?"

Eghan shook his head. "I have work to do here. I will see you at the evening meal."

She placed her hand on his and smiled. "Until then."

Ulhrik watched Eghan touch the spot where her hand had rested as he made his way back toward the room. He turned back and replaced the drawings on the table.

"Your impudence may get you into serious trouble again, Ulhrik," The prince said.

Ulhrik stopped unrolling the drawings. "So may your eagerness to please one with such charms and deceiving beauty."

Eghan's anger erupted. "I could have you dismissed. I could have you banished or ...."

Ulhrik leaned heavily on his walking stick and shook his head at him. As Eghan's voice trailed off, Ulhrik's tongue clicked. "We have no time for such foolishness."

Eghan took a deep breath and shook his head. He mumbled half to himself, "I fear I am being bewitched."

Ulhrik peered at him closely, then tapped the table with his stick. "Then get back to the work boy. That will clear your head."

Eghan nodded once and went outside. Laborers were busy hauling stone and mortar, carving beams and window casings. They took little notice of the young man as he peeled off his tunic and joined them. Ulrik sighed and turned to his work.

Journey Through Fire and Smoke

As Eghan worked through the morning, he was aware of a deep loneliness carving itself into him. A vision of Nara as he had last seen her floated before him and the loneliness became a physical ache. Nara's hair had grown to her shoulders again, after being cropped to disguise her identity when they entered Alinga territory. The day Eghan left for home, she rode with him as far as the fringes. He remembered how her hair shone with the iridescence of a raven's wing when she laid her head on his chest and said good-bye. He could still see her shining dark eyes. Nara, who shared his faith, who would understand what this building meant, who would support his desire to help build it. He wondered if Malora would do the same, if she knew... but something stopped his wondering. With a sudden surge of guilt, Eghan realized Malora's touch had jogged these memories. Shaking his head, he put his back into the work. *Ulhrik is right*, he thought, *we have no time for such nonsense.*

The old man was soon at his side and they worked together through the day, breaking only to drink now and then. Often they studied the drawings and each time Eghan followed Ulhriks gnarled finger as it traced the lines on the paper, he was in awe of the craftsman. They were in fact building a house within a house, one that was open with vaulted ceilings, the other hidden, closed away behind walls that moved and floors that opened into stairways. Many could live within it and never be seen.

****

As Malora rode back to the castle, alone in the carriage, she brooded. She knew the prince was holding something back from her. It is obvious his heart is not free, she thought. She settled back on the seat and smiled. I must discover who has bound it, and destroy her.

****

Nara stood still and listened. The music had stopped and the people had begun to cheer again, not waiting for Burke to speak. She glanced through the curtain that divided the room from the balcony on which he stood, and smiled. He waved the cheers into silence at last, and his voice boomed out.

"My friends..."

The cheers erupted again. Nara giggled with Brynna. "They are not being very polite."

Brynna opened the curtain slightly and peered out. "They are so happy, m'lady, every word is reason to cheer."

Burke raised his hand and began again. "We are here to crown our Queen...."

Once more the cheers interrupted him. Nara saw him turn to Adlair and say something, his hands outstretched. Adlair nodded and they both turned toward her, drawing back the curtain. She took Adlair's arm and stepped out. The crowd erupted, then began to chant, "Long live Queen Nara, long live the Queen."

Nara smiled and waved. In a few moments Adlair held up his hand and the people quieted.

"The Lord has done great things for us all. He has defeated our enemies and kept safe those whom he has chosen to lead. You have a heavy responsibility to protect the Queen He has given you, to obey her, to honor her, to pray for her." As he turned, the crowd cheered again until he began to address Nara directly, reading from The Book. "If you do away with the yoke of oppression, with the pointing finger and malicious talk, and if you spend yourselves on behalf of the hungry and satisfy the needs of the oppressed, then your light will rise in the darkness, and your night will become like the noonday. The Lord will guide you always; he will satisfy your needs in a sun-scorched land and will strengthen your frame. You will be like a well-watered garden, like a spring whose waters never fail. Your people will rebuild the ancient ruins and will raise up the age-old foundations; you will be called the Repairer of Broken Walls, the Restorer of Streets with Dwellings." That is the word of our God from the book of Isaiah, chapter 58, verses 9b to 12.

Adlair turned and nodded to Gage. As he stepped forward carrying a golden crown on a velvet cushion, Brynna stepped in front of her and removed the small tiara from her head. Adlair took the cushion from Gage's hands as Burke moved forward. The two Alingans lifted it and held it above Nara's head. Burke's voice rang out. "By the authoriry given us by God and the Alingan people, we crown you Queen of The Alingan Territory and all therein." After placing the crown on her head, Gage turned to the people and cried out, "Long live Queen Nara!"

The chant was raised once again. Music was struck and the people danced in the streets.

Nara watched them for a while, then stepped forward and raised her hand. It took a while for the people to realize she intended to speak. When they finally began to quiet, Nara raised her voice.

"This day has made me more happy than I could have imagined." The crowd cheered.
"It is a great gift, to be given the leadership of a great people. I pledge to you now that I will do everything in my power to maintain peace and prosperity in The Alingan Territory." Again cheers erupted until Nara held up her hand. "But I cannot do this alone. I need your help, the help of every man, woman and child. I ask that you make the same pledge, for the prosperity of our kingdom." The faces peering up at her nodded and their expressions became more sober. Nara turned and nodded to Gage. The general stepped out.

"Repeat after me. We, the Alingan people." He stopped, waiting for the words to be echoed back to him. "Pledge our allegiance to Queen Nara." The voices swelled as the words were repeated. "We pledge to uphold the law, and maintain the peace."

Nara's hand tightened on Adlair's arm. He turned

to her and smiled as he continued. "And to pray for one another and for our Queen."

Nara stepped forward and raised her hand as she said the final word. "Amen."

The amen echoed back, then the cheering, as the small group left the balcony.

Chapter Eleven

Eghan heard the howls as he approached the stables on his way home. At first he thought it was an animal, but as he broke into a run, he remembered hearing a similar sound before, in an Alingan village. It was a child, screaming in pain. The stable-master had his back to him, so Eghan could not tell who was being beaten, but it did not matter. He grabbed the man's arm as it came up, a strip of braided leather swinging from his hand. The man wrenched his arm loose and whirled around. Recognizing him immediately, he dropped to one knee, his head bowed, his voice trembling. "Prince Eghan."

Eghan pushed past him. "I will not tolerate this..." He stopped, catching his breath as he looked down at the boy curled into a ball at his feet. "Latham." In a moment he was on his knees beside the boy. Then he stood and turned on the stable-master. "How dare you strike my page?"

"Page, m' lord? I did not know he was your page, Prince Eghan, I swear it. Yesterday he was a stable boy, m'lord, and a lazy one at that. I thought ..."

"You thought what?"

"I...I thought he'd stolen the fine clothes he's wearin', m'lord. That's why I was thrashin 'im. I...I thought 'e was lyin', m'lord." The man dropped the leather strap and fell down before him. "Forgive me, Prince Eghan. I did not know he belonged to you."

Eghan picked up the piece of leather and stared down at the man, anger surging inside him. He brought his arm back, but stopped and threw the strap to the ground.

"Beat a child like that again and I will see you dismissed. Get out of my sight before I order it now."

The man scrambled to his feet and fled without looking back.

Eghan bent down to help Latham stand. "Come. I will have someone tend to you."

"Oh, I'm all right, m'lord." The boy bobbed to his feet. "He was just gettin' started."

Eghan's eyebrows shot up. "From the way you were howling I would have thought he was torturing you."

Latham grinned. "The yowlin' sometimes makes 'em stop sooner, m'lord."

Eghan shook his head. "Perhaps I should have let him continue for a while."

"My oh my, no, m'lord. That was enough to last me fer months."

Eghan sighed. "You do seem to have a knack for getting yourself into trouble, Latham. Why were you here, in the stables?"

"I came to check on Ezra, to make sure they was lookin after 'im."

"Ah, yes." Eghan cocked his head. "And to flaunt your new position perhaps?"

The boy dropped his eyes.

Eghan sighed. "And are they looking after Ezra?"

"Yes, melord. He's lookin' fine."

"Good. Then you can concern yourself with me. I am in need of a hot bath. Run and see to it."

"Yes, m'lord, right away."

Eghan watched him run off and started to follow, then turned back into the stables. It had been a while since he had been there. He wandered slowly over the smooth cobblestones, listening to the horses nicker, smelling the odors of leather harness, enjoying the memories it brought to his mind. He was about to leave when he heard a voice that stopped him. A woman's voice.

He rounded a corner and almost ran into Duchess Malora, a young boy at her side. For the flash of a second, Eghan thought he read fear in the boy's face as he tucked something into his tunic. For a flash of a second, Eghan wondered at it. But as he began to ask, the duchess began to speak.

Malora laughed and gave a small curtsy. "After you, Prince Eghan."

Eghan smiled and bowed. "Ladies first, Duchess."

She ducked her head. "I was about to ask about your horses."

Eghan cocked his head. "I was about to ask why you were here."

"I was looking for a suitable mount to ride before dinner. I am bored with the horses my uncle brought with us. They are all so tame, so safe. I prefer an animal with a bit of spirit." She waved her hand at the boy. "This young man was helping me choose, but perhaps you could be of assistance?"

Eghan waved his hand at the boy, who dashed off after a quick glance at Malora. She slipped her arm through his and turned him in the other direction. "I am sure there are many horses here that would please me."

As Eghan guided her past Ezra's stall, the horse stamped and snorted. Malora stopped.

"What about this one?"

"This one is mine. His name is Ezra."

"Ezra? What an odd name."

"It is a very old name, taken from the Book of The One True God."

Malora's smile was almost a smirk. "I see. What does it mean?"

"Helper. Ezra was a priest who led his people after they rebuilt the temple of worship."

"A fitting name for your horse, then, Prince Eghan."

Eghan tried to shake the feeling the comment had been more of an insult than a compliment. As she reached to stroke Ezra's nose, the horse tossed his head. Eghan motioned toward a horse on the other side of the stable. "This one might be to your liking. He is spirited but quite easy to control, for one who knows how to ride."

Malora moved gracefully to his side and smiled. "Then he will be perfect. Will you join me?"

Eghan nodded. "It would be my pleasure. I will have them saddled immediately."

It felt good to be on Ezra again. It felt good to watch Malora ride, though when she was beside him her horse twitched with tension, making Ezra uneasy. Most of the time she was ahead of him, her hair streaming out behind her. They had ridden for some time when Eghan suggested they turn back. Malora lifted her head, then grinned at him as she turned her horse and trotted by. "I am hungry!"

Before Eghan could respond, her horse bolted. Ezra leaped forward instantly, almost throwing Eghan from his seat. He recovered quickly and they were soon neck and neck with the Duchess and her mount. Eghan was surprised, then a bit angry to see that the girl was laughing as they charged on. When they finally trotted into the courtyard, he leaped down and faced her.

"I thought your horse bolted, that you had lost control."

Malora laughed and again Eghan felt an uneasiness at the sound of it that only increased at the snap in her eyes.

"I never lose control, my prince. Never."

Eghan was about to respond to the mockery in her eyes when they suddenly changed, seeming almost to worship him. She placed her hand on his chest and smiled. "But thank you for your concern. I know I would always be safe with someone so eager to protect me." She stepped away. "Will you ride with me again, tomorrow?"

Eghan peered into her now earnest eyes. "Yes, of course."

Malora smiled brightly again. "Good. Now, I am famished, aren't you?"

Eghan became instantly aware of his rumbling stomach and remembered the bath he had told Latham to prepare. He bowed to the Duchess. "I would be honored to dine with you."

Chapter Twelve

Malora was brushing out her hair when she heard the tap on her door. She opened it a crack, then stood back as her uncle stepped in quickly, closing the door behind him.

"Well, what do you think of your prince, my dear?"

Malora peered into the mirror and resumed brushing her gleaming hair. "He has more...substance than I expected, and he is more handsome. I will admit, I find him almost attractive, Uncle." She watched the man's face reflected in the glass for a moment, then asked, "Does that upset you?"

Rian stepped close to her, placed both hands on her shoulders and pressed his thumbs into her flesh until she winced.

"Don't play your games, with me, Malora. Focus on your purpose here." He released her shoulders. "You do want your father to be proud of you, don't you?"

Malora's eyes flashed as she spat out, "He won't be

completely satisfied until I am betrothed to this ... weakling."

Rian laughed. "So, he is not your choice for a husband, in spite of his substance and good looks?" He waved his hand. "No matter. The marriage will be short, my dear. You know your father's plans once we are in control."

The young woman lifted her head, relishing the idea. "Yes. When this king and his son are dead, we will own it all. Then we will ride in strength back to Alinga Territory. That raven-haired wench will rue the day she returned." She whirled around, spread her arms wide, dancing around the room, laughing. "All of it, all of it will be ours."

Her uncle nodded, but shushed her. "Keep that always in your mind, Malora, but do not be too impatient. The boy may be a sop, but his father or one of the others may become suspicious if you push too hard. Let them come to you."

Malora waved her hand. "His father is so anxious to marry him off, it is very easy to charm him. We need fear no opposition there." She stepped to the window and looked out. "The guardian, though, may be a problem. I have caught him looking at me with an odd expression."

"Then it may be necessary to arrange an accident."

Malora smirked. "Perhaps. But remember what Father said. We must accomplish this with as little fuss and as much cunning as possible, to win the people to our side." She laughed and her eyes flashed as she turned to her uncle. "But you will get your chance to arrange whatever you wish, once I am queen.

When her uncle was gone, Malora stood for a time at the open window, gazing out past the courtyard to the countryside. The view was so different from the one she had known growing up. That view was grey and cold, interminable stretches of mountains and rock shrouded in mist and cloud. She drank in the rich green of this valley, the blackness of the earth being cultivated, the color of flowers blooming. She smiled. It will be mine, she thought, all of it will be mine.

****

Melora strode just ahead of Eghan, her head up, her hair loose and flowing. She wanted to sway with the movement of the ancient trees around her. She liked the fact that Eghan followed closely as they walked into the middle of one of the valley's finest orchards. They walked for some time without speaking before she stopped and turned to him. "I have never seen trees like these. I could walk here forever."

Eghan smiled. "This was one of my favorite places when I was a boy."

Malora peered at him, studying him, like a child studies a newly discovered insect. When she realized she was making the prince uncomfortable she smiled and watched him relax.

"It must have been wonderful, to have lived here as a child."

"What is your home like, Malora?"

She dropped her eyes and turned away from him. "My home was well suited to me, I suppose."

Eghan touched her arm. The lightness of it made her shiver just a bit. "You did not have a happy childhood?"

She shrugged slightly. "I was mostly in the company of old men." She shook herself. "But let's not dwell on gloomy thoughts. Tell me, what did you play here, as a child?"

Eghan grinned. "I used to hide in the highest branches and cause my guardian to shake with frustration."

Malora laughed, then glanced over her shoulder. Khalwyd had kept his distance, following slowly with their horses. "Have you done that, recently?" She made her eyes dance with mischief.

Eghan's grin widened. "Can you climb in that?"

Malora glanced down at her riding habit. "I will manage." She grabbed his hand and tugged him into a run. Within a few moments they heard Khalwyd call, but kept up the pace until they were well away from him. Eghan pointed to a large spreading tree with branches low enough to be reached from the ground. He was up and leaning down for her hand before Khalwyd was in sight. They climbed as high as they dared. Malora covered her mouth with her hand to stifle her laughter as Eghan's guardian walked directly below them. They watched as he wandered in the orchard for a while, calling Eghan's name, then stomped off in obvious frustration, leaving the horses to graze.

"You must have been a difficult child for those old men, Malora," Eghan said.

She knew he had said it in jest, but she did not laugh. She wanted to scowl, but did not want to invite more questions. She turned away and began climbing down before he could say anything more.

They reached the ground together and when she turned to face him, she smiled again. "Now, tell me, Prince Eghan, what did you do once you were alone?"

"I would ride wherever I wanted, often toward the mountains at the northern end of the valley."

"Wonderful!" She whirled and raced toward the horses. They rode side by side at a breakneck pace, but as the mountains loomed closer, Malora pulled her horse up and turned its head.

Eghan continued on a ways then sat his horse quietly. When he made no move to join her, Malora trotted up to him. The prince's gaze lingered on the tall barrier that closed off the end of the valley. Malora watched his face for a moment before speaking. "What are you thinking?"

Eghan seemed startled by the question. He lifted his chin toward the rock face before them. "When I was a boy I dreamed of what it might be like on the other side of these mountains. I was drawn to them, as though they held my destiny. Not long ago, I was taken there against my will. For a time, it was my home."

"Taken? By whom?"

"By a Huntsman. He was hired to take me to Alinga Territory, probably to be killed."

Malora made her eyes widen. "You must have been very frightened."

Eghan nodded. "At first, but the Huntsman did not do what he had been hired to do. He took me to a hidden valley instead, where I discovered I had an uncle, a man of considerable wisdom and power. He taught me a great deal and eventually I grew to be at peace there with him. I grew very fond of him and ... the others."

Malora leaned closer. "Others?"

"An Alingan princess also lived there. Her name is Nara."

Malora almost hissed at the way he said her name but she controlled herself. "And your uncle, what is his name?"

"Some call him The Wizard. The Huntsmen had their own name for him, the name he prefers, Adlair."

Melora turned her face away and tried not to let her tension show but when Eghan put his hand on her arm and spoke her name she could not contain herself. "I hate the mountains," she said and pulled hard on the reins. Her horse reared, then whirled and galloped away.

Eghan followed, and eventually Malora allowed him to catch up just as they neared the gates of his father's castle. As they dismounted, Eghan waved the servants away.

He took the reins of Malora's mount and gave a

slight bow. "I will tend to your horse, m'lady."

"You? Where is your boy? I would see him punished for not being here to meet you."

Eghan grinned. "Latham does neglect his duties at times, but he..." Before he could finish, the page raced toward them, breathless.

"Sorry, m'lord. I was uh...uh..." He dropped his head, took a deep breath, and said more quietly. "I forgot about ye."

Eghan shook his head and handed the boy the reins to the two horses. "Make sure they are well looked after, Latham."

"Oh my, yes, m'Lord." He took the reins and led the horses away at a trot. Eghan smiled as he watched him go.

Malora watched Eghan. When he turned back to her, she spoke quietly. "You treat him as though he were a member of your household, as though you cared about him."

Eghan seemed surprised at the comment, but did not hesitate in answering. "I do care about him. I think the Lord brought Latham to me for a special purpose, though, I admit at times I do wonder what it could possibly be."

Malora cocked her head. "The Lord? What Lord?"

"The One True God, The Lord I worship, Duchess."

She raised her head a notch. "Oh, yes. Well, you would think he could have sent you one that was more attentive."

Eghan laughed. "I have had attentive servants all my life. I would rather have one who is genuine in his affection than a hundred who act from duty alone."

As they walked away from the stables and into the castle, Malora pondered the words of this young prince. She wondered what it would be like to know such affection, to have even her servants display it toward her. Such a thing was beyond comprehending, yet this prince seemed to believe it was possible. She shook herself. I must remember my father's warning about this place, she thought. He said it might captivate me. He said I must keep my heart hard. Yes. That is the only way to victory here.

Chapter Thirteen

Eghan was standing at a window, leaning heavily against its frame and staring into space, when the boy burst in.

"M'Lord..."

He whirled around, frowning. "Latham, how many times have I told you not to burst in on me like that? Go back into the hallway and knock, and wait for my response."

"But, m'lord...."

"Now, or I swear I'll send you back to the stables."

Latham ducked his head and stepped back through the doorway. At the short rap Eghan turned back to the window, slowly put his foot up on the sill, placed his elbow on his knee and rested his chin in his hand. The rap came again, louder. Eghan did not move. He heard the door creak and spoke without turning.

"I did not respond yet, Latham."

"How long do you intend to keep us waiting?"

Eghan whirled around and stared. "Uncle!" In a heartbeat he was in the man's arms, laughing, almost crying. He looked up into his uncle's face as Adlair held him out at arm's length. "You do not

know how I have looked forward to this day,"
Eghan said.

"No more than I, Eghan, no more than I." He
grinned and half turned to the door where Latham
was peering in. "But one would think you intended
to wait a while longer."

Eghan rolled his eyes. "I do not know if I will ever
get the boy properly trained."

"I understand your frustration." Adlair's eyes
twinkled.

Eghan laughed and waved to the boy. "Come in,
Latham."

He stepped in, his grin foolish and awkward.
Eghan sobered and waved his hand.

"Do you know who this is?"

Latham shook his head. "But he gave me a piece o'
silver to bring him to ye, melord."

Eghan flashed a look at Adlair, who turned away
to hide his grin.

"A piece of silver? Is that all my life is worth to
you, boy?"

Latham's face crinkled into a frown. "Your life,
melord?"

"What if this man had intended to murder me?
You have just led him into my private chambers
without even knowing who he is."

The color drained from the boy's face. "I...I didn't
think ..."

Eghan's hands were on his hips. "Exactly."

"M'lord," Latham fell to his knees, tears brimming
in his eyes. "I would never let anyone hurt you."

Eghan sighed. "Get up Latham, I do not intend to punish you. Fortunately, this time we do not have to be concerned. This is my Uncle Adlair, my mother's brother."

As Latham stood, he stared up at the tall man, his jaw open. "Yr...you're the wizard?"

Adlair shook his head. "I am no wizard, boy."

Eghan took Latham's shoulder and pushed him gently toward the door. "Get my uncle some refreshments, Latham, and be quick about it."

The boy responded without taking his eyes off Adlair. "My, oh my, yes, m'lord."

He bumped into the door-frame before he finally turned and fled.

Eghan laughed with his uncle. "Surely I was not that bad?"

Adlair stroked his chin. "Well ..."

"Never mind. Come, sit down. Does my father know you have arrived?"

"Not yet. I was on my way to announce myself when I heard your young lad there telling one of the servants what a good page he was learning to be. I could not resist the opportunity to see you immediately. You look well, Eghan."

"You look tired, Uncle. Was the journey hard?"

"Not overly so, but I fear I am getting old." He stretched and arched his back, then sat. "These bones seem to ache more readily than they used to."

"How are things with ... with the Alingans?"

Adlair smiled. "Nara is well. She misses you."

Eghan knew he was blushing as Adlair continued.

"She said to tell you she is well, and thank you for the provisions. She was crowned Queen only a few weeks ago."

"And her people, are they accepting her?" Eghan knew his voice sounded too controlled.

"More than accepting. They would do anything for her."

Eghan rose and walked to the window. The silence made the ache he felt more intense. Shaking himself, he turned back and faced his uncle. "There has been no further trouble? No sign of Malnar's men?"

Adlair shook his head. "None. I would not have left her if I thought there were any danger."

Eghan gave a quick nod.

"How has it been for you here, since your return?"

Eghan came back to his chair. "At first it felt odd, as though I did not belong, but now it almost feels as though I had never left, that everything in the past year was a dream. I have been so occupied with the building and with ... other things, I suppose that accounts for it."

"Building?"

"Yes," Eghan got to his feet again. "We are building a house of prayer, Uncle, a place of worship and refuge."

"Refuge?"

As Eghan opened his mouth to explain, Latham kicked open the door with his heel and entered backwards carrying a heavy tray, talking as he came. "Yer refreshments, melords, looks good, don't they? Haven't eaten in a while meself, makes them cakes look fine. Smells good too, don't they? And the tea's hot. Pipin' hot and there's..."

"Latham!"

The boy stopped abruptly, the tray half on the table, and looked up innocently. "Yes, m'lord?"

Eghan sighed. "You may go."

"Oh." He glanced down at the food. "Go, m'lord?"

He started to slide his hand out from under the tray, realizing just in time that it was not yet sitting properly on the table. Shoving it forward, he took a small step back, still staring at it. His eyes flicked to Eghan's face for a moment, then back to the food.

Eghan rolled his eyes at Adlair again. "All right, boy. Take some with you and be gone."

Latham grinned, grabbed two biscuits and was out the door before Eghan could say another word.

Adlair was chuckling. "Where did you find him?"

Eghan gave him a wry grin, aware of the irony as he answered. "In the stables."

Adlair laughed outright and Eghan reached across to grasp his arm. "It is so good to have you here at last, Uncle. I have missed you."

"But you were saying you have been kept busy?"

"Yes." Eghan grew more serious. "Khalwyd and I have become stone builders since returning."

"You do not seem entirely happy with that."

Eghan paced the room while Adlair poured his own tea. He told his uncle about Ulhrik and his prophesy, about the house of prayer and its intended use. The words tumbled out and Eghan

realized as he spoke how good it was to release the
tension that had been building inside him. When he
was finished his uncle remained silent, his brow
furrowed as he stared down into the cup he held in
his hands. Eghan suddenly became aware of the
burden this would be to him.

"I am sorry, Uncle. I should have waited until you
had rested before spilling all this before you."

Adlair held up his hand. "It is just as well, Eghan. I
remember Ulhrik and the words of his prophesy. I
have often wondered what became of him." He
stood suddenly. "I must speak with your father
about these and other things."

Eghan headed for the door. "Yes, of course. I will
take you to him."

The king was alone in the great hall when they
found him. As they walked across the shining floor,
Eghan realized the significance of this moment.
These men had been raised as brothers, had become
brothers through marriage but had been estranged
for many years. Eghan smiled as he saw his father
grasp Adlair's arms and raise him up when he
bowed.

Gherin's voice was low. Eghan thought he heard a
hesitancy in it, but relaxed when his father said,
"Brother. It has been too many years."

Adlair stepped closer, embracing the king for a
few moments before stepping back to look into his
face. His voice was husky with emotion. "God is

good, so very good. Only His grace could have brought us together again at last."

The two men sat across from each other before the hearth and began to talk of the past. Eghan listened as they relived their boyhood, the days before Eghan's mother, the queen, died, and the time since. He was struck again as his father told how he had accepted The One True God, how he wished to restore and rebuild the relationships he had been afraid of in the past. Eghan was pleased to see him nod as Adlair talked of the terms of trade with the Alingans.

The night was almost breaking into dawn before they began to discuss the prophesy. Adlair did not speak, but nodded as Gherin told him what was being done and how he felt.

"I have prayed earnestly that God would spare my people, Adlair. I confess there are moments when I am so filled with dread I can barely function."

Eghan was amazed to hear his father talk of his fear so openly. He thought to lay his hand on his father's arm, but held back.

Adlair leaned forward. "We must hold on to what we know, Gherin. God is good, whatever His answers may be."

Gherin nodded, leaned forward and grasped both of Adlair's arms as they rose together. "I hope you will stay with us, Adlair, at least for a time. We have need of your wisdom."

"I was hoping you would extend that invitation, Gherin. It would give me great pleasure to remain in this house once again." He smiled as he glanced at Eghan. "I have become quite attached to your son."

Gherin raised his eyebrows, but smiled back. "So I have come to understand. I am sure Eghan will be pleased to have you here."

Eghan grinned through a yawn. "As long as he does not insist I chop enough wood for the whole house and clean every stall in the stables."

Adlair laughed. "It would seem you have enough to do, without my adding more chores."

The king's face changed. "We must discuss the prophesy in more depth, brother, but now I think we all need some sleep before the new day is upon us."

As Eghan and his uncle strode from the room, he glanced back and thought he saw Gherin's eyes darken as Adlair rested his arm easily across his shoulder.

Chapter Fourteen

Nara smiled as Gage waved the papers in his hand. "This is good news for our people, my lady."

She nodded. "Yes. And the terms are quite generous. King Gherin is proving to be as good as his word."

"Food and goods from the Valley of Lhin for ore from our mines. We must increase production immediately."

Nara raised her eyes to his. "Yes, but make sure the safety precautions are followed, Gage. I don't want to hear of men dying in the mines just so we can trade with the Lhinians."

Gage bowed. "I will see to it."

Nara sighed as she watched him leave the room. She knew increasing the production in the mines was a good thing for them all, yet she wished it did not have to be. Mining was a dangerous business and even with the safety precautions she knew some would die in those deep dark places. She stepped out onto the balcony that overlooked the square. It had become a bustling place once again, the whipping post removed and the people free to buy and sell as they wished. Once trade was established with the Lhinians the marketplace would be even more busy and the people more prosperous.

Nara knew King Gherin's generous agreement was likely Adlair and Eghan's doing and smiled briefly, knowing they were thinking of her and her people. But there had been no note, no message to her personally with the document she had shown Gage. She sighed again. For so it must be.

She stepped to a small desk in the corner of the room and picked up a gold embossed envelope. The flowing script of the message inside was also written in gold, the words formal.

To Queen Nara of the Alinga Territories

An invitation

from the court of King Delmar Ul,

Your presence is respectfully requested

at the presentation of

Her Royal Highness, Princess Talwynn Ul

on the occasion of her fifteenth birthday.

When she had first read the note Nara had a fleeting thought that she was reading a message addressed to another. Seeing Queen Nara in writing gave her pause. But that was who she was now – a queen with responsibilities and duties. Nara glanced again at the date. Only three weeks away.

She replaced the card in the envelope and put it down with another sigh. She knew these invitations would come now that she was queen, but she did not look forward to them. She would be like a curiosity on display in the courts of their neighbours, and no doubt the focus of much whispered gossip and perhaps much mockery. With only one suitable gown to wear, she would have to appear dressed like a peasant much of the time. But she knew it would be wise to accept this invitation and to take the opportunity to solidify relations with the Brimleish.

Nara looked down at herself, then stepped to the long looking-glass in her chamber. She sighed. Well, let them laugh, she thought. If I can secure an alliance that will benefit my people, their disdain will not matter.

Chapter Fifteen

Malora stiffened as Adlair's imposing figure entered the great hall. She had felt uneasy when she heard Eghan's uncle had arrived. Now, in his presence, she was finding it difficult to control her anxiety. The man was striding toward them, his keen eyes taking in everything in the room. She felt like fleeing but steeled herself to undergo his scrutiny.

As though her uncle had read her mind, he leaned toward her and whispered in her ear. "Remember your father's words when we parted, Malora." She remembered them well. "Be sweet and charming, my dear," her father had said. "They will be drawn into your web before they know what has happened." Her smile began as a smirk but she skillfully made it brighten, made her eyes widen with feigned innocence. Her confidence renewed, she turned to face this Lord Adlair as King Gherin led him toward them.

Gherin reached for her hand, then turned to Adlair as she and her uncle rose from the table.

"May I present Duchess Malora, and her uncle,

Lord Rian Gille, honored guests in my house. Lord Rian, Duchess, this is my brother-in-law, Lord Adlair."

Malora curtsied gracefully before him but quickly averted her eyes as she stood erect. Her uncle spoke up, diverting Adlair's attention.

"We have heard much about you, Lord Adlair. Is it all true, or have you allowed truth to be spun into myth?"

Gherin cleared his throat. "The people love to exaggerate, as I am sure you know, Lord Rian, but many of the stories you have heard, though amazing, are indeed true."

Rian Gille's mouth jerked into a smirk. "So the Wizard of Lhin is real, after all."

Malora noticed Adlair did not smile as he replied. "I am but a servant of The One True God, Lord Rian."

"Ah yes, so I understand. Well, each to his own god, as they say."

Servants entered with platters of food, and the group was seated.

As the conversation flowed around the table, Melora watched Adlair and Eghan out the corner of her eye. She noted that the prince's eyes rarely left his uncle's face. He adores him, she thought. And that must change.

Her thoughts were interrupted when Adlair addressed her directly.

"Was your journey to the Lhin valley a long one, Duchess Malora?"

She smiled her sweetest smile and answered. "Not overly long, no. Thank you for asking, Lord Adlair." She lowered her eyes as his sought them. "But it was rather boring."

"You did not enjoy travelling through the various villages and farmlands?"

"One village looks much like the next and one cow is as unremarkable as all the rest." She raised her eyes to his and wondered what he was trying to discern from such questions.

Adlair smiled at her. "Well I am sure your time here, in my brother-in-law's court will be more to your liking."

"I am liking it here," she said, and felt the pull of truth in her own words. She almost added, "and I intend to stay," but caught herself just in time and turned away from Adlair. This wizard is dangerous, she thought. We must be rid of him.

****

Eghan picked at his food and tried to shake himself out of the gloominess he had been feeling since Adlair arrived. The news that Nara was now queen of the Alinga had shaken him, more than he expected. He realized he had been secretly hoping something would happen to prevent her coronation. But it had taken place, her future was now well set into the tradition of nobility and leadership in Alinga Territory. *Nara is queen of the Alinga,* Eghan repeated to himself. *And I will some day be king of my father's realm. Nara will never be a part of my future.*

"Prince Eghan?"

He turned to find himself gazing into Malora's soft eyes.

"I ... I am sorry, Duchess, I did not hear you."

She smiled. "You were too far away to hear any of us, it would appear. May I be so bold as to ask where you were?"

"Brooding on gloomy thoughts I am afraid, but I will try to be better company for the rest of the meal."

The girl placed a hand gently on his arm. "I think you have been working too hard, Eghan. Ride with me in the morning?"

He nodded. "It would be my pleasure, as always, Duchess."

Malora pursed her lips. "Eghan, I am offended!"

Eghan turned his full attention to her. "Offended?"

"We have been friends for some time now. I would have thought you would do me the courtesy of addressing me by my name, not my title." Her eyes teased as she cocked her head slightly to one side.

"Forgive me, Du ... Malora."

She laughed and Eghan found himself smiling in spite of the heaviness that still tugged at him.

"That's better. Now, I know you do not like being up with the birds, so shall we ride just before breakfast and make them wait for us?"

Eghan grinned at the mischief in her eyes. "My father is not a patient man."

"Oh, but he would not chide a guest, now would he?"

Eghan glanced at his father. He had seen how the king's eyes shone when he watched her. "I know he would never chide you, Malora. Choose your time, we will ride whenever you wish."

The dinner finally ended and Eghan slipped away from Malora and the entourage. His mind was swirling as he headed for his chambers and he leaped back when Adlair stepped out of a side corridor. When his heart rate slowed he grinned at his uncle. "No wonder they call you a wizard, Uncle, when you appear out of nowhere like that."

Adlair did not smile back at him. His brow was furrowed and his voice deep when he spoke.

"I have been watching you and the young Duchess with a rising sense of unrest, Eghan. It is obvious you are taken with her and equally obvious the girl is using every trick she knows to make it so."

Eghan opened his mouth to respond but stopped when Adlair raised his hand and continued.

"I also noticed your father studied her with admiration. The king's eyes often drifted toward the girl and as he watched her, a smile played on his mouth. The girl is dangerous, Eghan. It would be best if you tell your father you have no interest in her and ask that she and her uncle be dismissed immediately."

Eghan was stunned by his uncle's words. "You presume a great deal, Uncle," he said, making no attempt to hide the irritation he felt. "And my father is not likely to listen to such a request even if I did agree to make it. He is determined that I should court the Duchess. To be honest I was against the plan at first, mostly because I resented being told who to court, but as you say, she is a beguiling young woman and I am taken with her."

Eghan pushed away a prodding to listen to his uncle. He was weary of everyone telling him what to do and when.

"What do you know about her and her uncle?" Adlair leaned toward him. "Where have they come from?"

Eghan frowned as he realized he did not know and annoyed that he would have to admit it. "I am sure my father knows everything about them, Uncle. He has been trying to seal an alliance with her people for some time, so I have been told." Eghan half turned and began to walk away. "Speak to my father about the Duchess and her lineage. I am sure you will find it is all in good order."

"Have you been studying The Book, Eghan?"

Eghan stopped for a moment, but did not turn back. He strode away without answering, feeling Adlair's eyes on him. He shrugged off the uneasy feeling that churned in his stomach. *My uncle plays too much upon his reputation,* he thought. The look in Malora's eyes when she asked him to call her by her first name swam in his mind and blocked all else.

Chapter Sixteen

Malora had never seen her uncle so agitated. He was almost spitting the words at her.

"This man could disrupt everything. We must move more quickly. You must pull the prince into your web, Malora, and soon."

"He is already in it, Uncle, but it will take time to completely ensnare him. Besides, I do not want to rush."

Rian Gille lunged at her, grasping her arms until she winced. "It must be done. You must be wed before this wizard can interfere."

She tried to pull free of his grasp. "If you feel he is such a danger to us, perhaps you should arrange one of your 'accidents.' "

The man stared at her. "He is a danger to us, Malora and you should recognize it and be anxious to remove the danger." His eyes narrowed. "Or is your allegiance being swayed by this handsome boy and his doting father?"

Malora scoffed. "Don't be ridiculous. My ambitions do not stop at being the bride of this prince, Uncle. I am my father's daughter."

Rian released her. "Remember what he expects of you, what he expects of us both." He paced the room. "An accident may be..." He stood very still, then smirked and spoke more slowly. "No. I think it will be more expedient to arrange something else."

"What do you mean?"

"Your winning charm must be at its peak, my dear, for this to succeed, but I have confidence in you. As you say, you are your father's daughter."

****

Malora took extra care with her grooming as she prepared to meet the prince the next morning. She was pleased with her new riding habit. The rich blue color made her eyes vibrant. As she rubbed scented water into her hair, she lifted her chin, smiled into the glass and whispered, "Come My Prince, and be dazzled. It is time for the spider to poison the fly."

Catching her reflection in the glass as she passed it, she stopped, turned back and peered at herself. She was almost surprised at the glint of sadness lingering in her eyes, but allowed her self to feel it. "My prince," she whispered again, "Oh, beware, my prince."

****

Eghan was aware that his heart was racing as Malora slipped her hand through his arm. She leaned just slightly toward him, her head cocked to the side as she looked up at him. He was almost afraid to meet her eyes. When he did, he stopped breathing.

Malora smiled. "I want to ride like the wind today, Eghan. I am feeling ... I don't know, excited, for some reason. Aren't you?"

Eghan found himself nodding. "We will ride past the orchards, if you like, and along the river. It is a good place to let the horses run."

She leaned closer and put her other hand on his. "Wonderful!"

Eghan caught the scent of her perfume and leaned down toward her. She smiled and lifted her face.

Their lips were just about to touch when Latham burst around the corner of the stable, talking as he came. "Ezra's ready to go, melord. More than ready, he's anxious, snorting like a dragon, he is, and..."

Eghan jerked back and stared at him. Latham looked from the Duchess to his master. His eyes widened and a red flush crept up his neck, over his ears and into his cheeks. Eghan could feel the same thing happening to him.

"Woo..would you like me to come with ye, today, m'lord?"

Malora swept by him, glaring at the boy as she grasped the riding crop that had dangled from her wrist. She leaned toward Latham and spoke. Eghan could not hear her words but Latham's eyes went even wider and he took a step back. Eghan saw him swallow hard. "Ye...yes, melady." He whirled around and ran.

Malora turned back to Eghan and took his hand. "We do not need company, do we, Eghan?" She smiled and led him along behind her.

They rode for the entire morning, at first keeping a furious pace. Malora often charged on ahead, then came swooping back, her hair a golden stream behind her, her face flushed, her smile flashing. Later they walked along the river for a time, Malora slipping her arm through Eghan's or holding his hand. When she spoke her voice was light and eager.

"I cannot tell you how wonderful it has been to be here, Eghan, and to have the pleasure of your company. I shall be quite unhappy to leave."

Eghan stopped short. "But you are not thinking of leaving so soon, surely?" His thoughts flew, wondering if Adlair had spoken to his father and convinced him to dismiss them from his court.

Malora's eyes were almost pleading. "My uncle is beginning to talk of it. He is a restless and impatient man." She stepped in front of him, averting her eyes and placing a hand on his chest. "I am glad you do not want me to leave, Eghan."

"I...no...I do not want you to leave."

She smiled up at him and took a step closer. He leaned down toward her. This time there was no interruption as their lips met. Eghan suddenly stepped back, blinking down at her. "I ... I ... forgive me, my lady ... I ..."

She stepped toward him again and placed her fingers on his lips. "Hush, my prince." Then her hand slipped to the back of his neck and slowly drew his head down.

****

Eghan was surprised to see Adlair standing at his door when he returned to his room. He dropped his eyes, remembering their last encounter. When his uncle did not speak, Eghan looked up. "I apologize for my disrespect when we last spoke, Uncle," he said.

Adlair put a hand on his shoulder. "I thought perhaps we could study The Book together this morning."

"I would like that, but I was just about to leave to see how the building of the House of Prayer is progressing. Would you like to join me?"

Adlair hesitated, then nodded. "I would," he said simply.

The whispers flew as Eghan and Adlair walked out among the people. Eghan caught a few of them as they went: "It's the wizard. The wizard has come back!" Now and then there was a quick intake of breath. A mother clutched her child close as she turned away.

Eghan knew his uncle had noticed. He spoke quietly as they walked toward the house of prayer. "They still fear you, Uncle."

Adlair nodded. "Fear and suspicion do not

relinquish their grip easily."

"We must do something to change that."

Adlair smiled and placed a hand on his shoulder. "Those I care most about have changed and no longer fear me, Eghan, that is a great comfort to me."

They were standing in front of the House of Prayer now, and as Eghan turned to enter it, he was surprised at the amount of work that had been done. With a slight pang of conscience, he realized it had been a long while since he had been there to help. They had not gone far when that fact was brought to his attention.

"Well, well, the prince returns at last. Thought you'd gone soft on me, boy. There's work needing to be done. Work you should be here to see accomplished. And where is that strong guardian of yours? Sloughing off as usual?"

Eghan smiled and waited for the tirade to be over. When Ulhrik stopped for a breath, Eghan waved his hand toward Adlair.

"Ulhrik, this is..."

"I know who he is, boy. Do you think I'm daft?" He waved his stick at Adlair. "Is this what has been keeping you from the work, or is it that pretty one with the enticing smile?"

Eghan's grin changed quickly to a frown. "Do not go too far, Ulhrik or ..."

"It is not I who should be cautious, young prince, not I." The old man turned and took a step away from them, talking to Adlair over his shoulder.

"Well, since you are here, I might as well show you what we have done. It will be good that you know the plan of this place."

Adlair fell into step with him and Eghan started to follow.

Ulhrik stopped him. "Not you. You have work to do. Git."

He waved his stick and Eghan sighed but turned away and went in search of the building foreman. It would be good to work for a few hours. Perhaps it would help to clear his mind of the conflicting thoughts that filled it like a massive cobweb.

****

Ulhrik led Adlair through the interior of the house, pointing out hidden passages behind walls that moved and stairways that led to tunnels that were almost complete. Then he led him into the main room, a large open sanctuary.

Adlair stopped at its centre and peered up into the high arches above him. "A fitting place for worship. You have done well, Ulhrik. Very well."

Ulhrik ignored the compliment, his stick tapping on the stone as he made his way to a narrow door. Adlair followed him through it and up a narrow spiralling stairway. The stairs curved steeply upwards, an open window every dozen steps, until they stopped at a high rampart. The wind was blocked as they stepped out onto a flat stone slab circled by thick walls with four large wooden beams forming an open roof.

"This will be enclosed soon," he explained, staring up. "It is designed to be a prayer cell." Ulhrik turned to Adlair, his eyes searching the man's face. "But it will be many years before it will be used for prayer. It will soon have another purpose. Soon it will be a cell of captivity." He leaned against the wall, still watching Adlair intently. Then he put all of his strength against one of the stones. It moved outward almost imperceptibly. Adlair met Ulhrik's eyes and nodded.

Ulhrik looked out over the courtyards, to the green fields and orchards of the Valley of Lhin. He took a deep breath. "It will not be long. It has already begun," he said. "We may not have time to finish what the king had planned for this house, but we have almost finished my plan and it is the more important, for now."

Adlair's eyes clouded. "Eghan will survive?"

Ulhrik nodded. "Yes. The prince of Lhin will survive."

****

Eghan was weary as he made his way to his chambers after the evening meal. The work on the House of Prayer had stiffened his muscles. I should get back into the routine of the work, he thought. But with the demands of his father presurring him to be in court, and to spend time with Malora, he did not see how that would be possible. His head was down, his mind so occupied that he did not see the Duchess coming toward him until he almost collided with her.

He jerked back. "Forgive me, Malora," he blurted. She smiled up at him and stepped closer. Eghan stepped away. "I have just come from the building and I have not yet washed."

Malora smiled. "That does not concern me. But I am concerned about you, Eghan."

"Concerned? Why?"

"You seem so preoccupied and even gloomy at times." She rested her hand on his chest. "I wish there was something I could do to help you be free of your worries."

Eghan sighed. "Easier said than done, I am afraid."

"But what is it that makes you so downcast, my friend?"

Eghan peered into her blue eyes and suddenly could think of nothing to say.

Malora stepped closer and let her head tip slightly to the side. "Perhaps you just need someone to comfort you," she said, "someone who will make you forget all the worries of the world.

Eghan dropped his head toward her inviting lips. As his lips met hers, his head swam. *This must be what it feels like to give in to drowning,* he thought. When Malora stepped back he was almost gasping.

She laughed, then took his hand. "Come. There is something I want to show you."

As though in a dream, Eghan found himself running with her as she led the way through the corridors to her own chambers. Suddenly she was once again in his arms. The fire that surged inside him made his head pound. He did not realize they were on the bed until the door to her room burst open. Eghan heard Malora cry out as she pulled away from him, threw herself on her uncle's chest and began to weep.

Eghan leaped up, his eyes locking on the deep and angry eyes of his father, the king.

Chapter Seventeen

Khalwyd paced. King Gherin sat with his head in his hands while Silhas stood silently beside him.

"I did not trust her from the moment I saw her." Khalwyd's voice was almost a growl. "There is something more here than meets the eye, Sire, I would stake my life on it."

The king stood to his feet. "I know what I saw, Khalwyd. We have no choice but to salvage what honor my son has left. He will marry her immediately."

"No!"

Khalwyd whirled around to see Adlair striding toward them.

"It would be a grave mistake to force a marriage, Gherin."

The king glared at his brother-in-law. "This is none of your concern, Adlair." He turned away and lowered his voice. "And there is no alternative."

"Put aside your pride, brother," Adlair said. "Your son's future is at stake, and perhaps much more."

"You would have Lord Rian and the Duchess leave this castle, bringing disgrace to our name?

That has occurred too often in my family."

Khalwyd was relieved that Adlair chose to ignore the jibe. "Eghan has sworn he did not violate the girl," he said.

Gherin waved his hand in the air. "Do you think that will matter once the rumors begin? It will destroy everything we have worked so hard to build for the last year. How can my son lead his people into an era of fellowship with The One True God if they even suspect he has shamed himself?"

Silhas raised his voice. "How can he lead his people with a wife who is full of deceit and trickery?"

The king sank down into his chair, his words almost a moan. "There is no other choice!"

Adlair reached his side and was about to speak again when Eghan stepped into the room.

"My Father is right. I will marry Malora." He raised his eyes to his father's face, wincing at what he saw there. "I ... I cannot expect your forgiveness, Father, but know that I did not intend ..."

"Intentions have little consequence in the face of actions, Eghan." The king's face softened. "But I am relieved that you have agreed to do what you must."

Khalwyd stepped forward, but the King raised his hand as he stood. "See that the preparations are made, Khalwyd and do it quickly."

"But, Sire..."

Gherin's look silenced him. He bowed and stepped back.

As the king turned to go, Adlair's voice was soft but strong. "This is a mistake, my brother."

Gherin's step hesitated, but he did not reply.

****

Latham burst into Eghan's chamber, gasping for breath.

Eghan caught his shoulders as the boy almost collapsed. "Latham, what is it? What's happened?"

The boy took two huge gulps of air. "There's hundreds of 'em, m'Lord, hundreds."

"Hundreds of what, Latham, what are you saying?"

"They're all in black, shields flashin like black lightenin'. I saw 'em, m'Lord. I did! I was off in the hills and I saw 'em comin'."

"There is no reason to be alarmed. My father always travels with his army."

Eghan stood erect at the sound of Malora's voice. "Your father? But I thought..."

"Really, Eghan, you are such a simple fool." She swept into the room, her smile sending a cold chill down Eghan's spine. "Just because I travelled here with my uncle does not mean I have no father."

"What else have you not told me about your family, Malora?"

The girl laughed. Eghan's hands clenched into fists.

"You will know what you need to know, soon enough." She whirled around and left the room.

Latham looked up at his master. "I am afraid, m'Lord, very afraid."

Eghan gripped the boy's shoulder. "Come. You must tell my father what you have seen."

When Eghan explained, the king frowned down at Latham. "Are you sure of what you saw, boy?"

The lad appeared to be too frightened to speak but nodded vigorously.

Khalwyd put his hand to his sword. "I will have our troops stand ready, Sire."

Gherin held up his hand. "We do not want to offend, Khalwyd. It is natural for Malora's father to come for the ceremony, though it is customary to wait for the invitation." His frown deepened. "Tell the men to be alert, but show no signs of aggression."

Khalwyd nodded and left the room.

It was late afternoon when the army arrived. Latham had not exaggerated. "I estimate five hundred men, at least," Khalwyd said as he and Eghan stood on the ramparts and watched the men make camp outside the castle walls. Eghan noticed every man was well armed, every horse covered in war blankets.

"They do not look friendly," Khalwyd commented.

Eghan remained silent as a small group

approached the castle gates on horse-back. The arrogant demeanor of the one who led the way was evident even from so far away. Eghan felt Khalwyd's hand on his shoulder. "We should be with the king."

Gherin had dressed in his finest robes. His sword rested visibly on his hip and he held his scepter in hand as the doors to the great hall swung open and Malora's father was announced.

"Duke Damon Gille."

Eghan noted there was nothing further, no realm, no position, just the man's name and the common designation of Duke. The name made Eghan's blood run cold. As Damon strode forward, Eghan remembered the presence of evil he felt when he was fighting for his life with Duke Malnar. His hand automatically went to the hilt of his sword.

Damon halted a few steps from the dais and gave a quick bow. When he stood erect Eghan was struck with the resemblance between father and daughter. This man was as handsome as Malora was beautiful. They had the same ice blue eyes.

"I understand we are soon to be related."

Eghan felt his father's anger. "A future relative does not usually arrive at the door with an army behind him, nor enter his court and address him with such disrespect."

Damon waved his hand as though to dismiss the comment. "It is not safe beyond your borders, Gherin Lhin. I am accustomed to travelling with a small part of my army at all times. I ask your pardon if it has troubled you."

Damon's eyes moved from one to another as he spoke, settling for a moment on Khalwyd, then on Eghan. Before the King had a chance to respond, he spoke again.

"Am I to assume this is my new son?"

Eghan gave a stiff bow. His hand did not leave his sword.

Damon took a few quick steps and before anyone could move he stood before Eghan, his eyes boring into him. It took every ounce of courage Eghan possessed to remain where he was and meet that gaze. His stomach churned. For a moment he thought he might vomit and he wondered if the man was going to strike him. But Damon smiled. "You are just as my daughter described in her letters."

Khalwyd moved closer and Damon's attention was diverted to him.

"And this is the guardian." His voice was flat. "I see you attend to your job. I trust my daughter will now be included in that protection."

Before Khalwyd could respond, Damon whirled around to the king. "I realize you have not had much time to ready rooms for us, Gherin..."

Eghan sucked in his breath at the obvious discourtesy as the man called his father by his given name. He saw the king's jaw clench but he responded evenly.

"The servants will show you to your quarters. I am sure you will find them adequate."

"Then we will retire to them." Damon gave another quick bow, turned on his heel and strode from the room.

Khalwyd's anger boiled over. "The gall of the man!"

The king waved a hand and a servant came close. "Summon Adlair and Silhas to my chambers immediately." He turned to Khalwyd. "Come. We must talk."

When they were all assembled, it was Khalwyd who spoke first. "I say throw them out on their ears."

"And risk war?" Silhas' forehead was furrowed as he spoke."You have seen his army, Khalwyd, and no doubt what lies at our gates is only a small part of it, as he has said."

Adlair spoke slowly. "It is not only war we should fear from Damon Gille. The man is controlled by evil. I felt it the moment he stepped through the castle gates."

Eghan peered at his uncle. "What does he want here?"

"Evil wants only one thing. To destroy."

"It is not too late to send them packing." Khalwyd was on his feet. "Let me rouse the guard, Sire. We will deliver this Lord Damon to his hounds and be rid of them."

The king shook his head. "I cannot give that order, Khalwyd. His daughter is betrothed to my son. She is, for all intents and purposes, now a member of my household."

Khalwyd tried to object again, but Gherin held up his hand as he looked at Eghan. "I am bound to protect Malora, and her family."

Khalwyd scowled. "I'll wager her family would not be bound by such a duty."

Gherin's frown deepened. "The wedding will go forward as planned."

Eghan almost groaned at the look in his father's eyes.

****

Eghan did not see Malora or her father again until the day of the ceremony. The great hall had been decorated, the lords and nobles of the realm assembled for the event. He stood beside the king, dressed in a dark tunic draped with the prince's golden sash, waiting for the Duchess and her father to appear. When they stepped forward, Eghan could not help but stare. Malora was dressed in a long white gown sewn with jewels and lace. Once again her beauty took his breath away. For a moment, when she raised her eyes to his, his heart filled with hope. Then she glanced at her father and the look they exchanged made Eghan's heart turn cold. When Malora looked at him again, there was no love there, no sign even of affection, only an icy stare of victory.

As their vows were exchanged, Eghan's spirit writhed within him. Those times over the past months when he had sensed Malora's duplicity surged up now in one strong sense of evil. As he pledged to care for and protect this woman, all of his being revolted against even being near her. He could not force himself to look at her again. As his father declared their marriage sealed before God, Eghan knew what they had just done was terribly wrong. Through trickery and deceit Malora had trapped him, and now he was lying to his people before God. He wanted to scream and run from the mockery of this ceremony, but he stood beside his beautiful bride as his people cheered and danced in the streets.

Chapter Eighteen

Nara tried not to reveal what she was feeling but she feared it was plain on her face. She turned away from Brynna, her hand shaking as she let the letter fall to the table.

"My lady?" Brynna stepped closer. "Is there something wrong?"

The words in Adlair's letter poured through her mind again and she took a deep breath before answering. "Yes, I fear there is, Brynna, but there is nothing that can be done." She turned and tried to smile at her handmaid. "Please tell Gage I must speak with him."

Brynna gave a quick curtsie and turned to leave. Nara called her name. "Ask Burke to attend as well."

When the general and Burke entered, she handed them the letter and watched their faces change as it was read. When Burke raised his head she wanted to throw herself into his arms and weep. But she did not.

"Unsettling news, my queen," he said, stepping

closer. "But we must trust that God's will is being done, even though it may seem..."

She nodded but turned away, trying not to let her voice betray her. "Yes. We must trust that His plan is best."

"Trusting is sometimes painful."

Nara dropped her head, fighting the tears that threatened to slip down her face. She heard Burke take another step toward her and felt his hand on her shoulder. She shook her head and straightened her shoulders.

"I am queen of my people, Burke, and my duty is clear. I must focus on that, and that alone."

"But even a queen must be allowed to weep when she is so full of sorrow." Burke's voice was so gentle it almost made her sob.

Nara whirled around and allowed his arms to engulf her as she wept on his chest. She gave in to the sorrow for only a few moments, then pulled away.

"Thank you, my friend," she said, "but I am not a child and there are other things to be concerned with." She stepped to her secretary's desk and picked up the small gold embossed envelope. "I received another letter a few days ago." She handed it to Gage. "An invitation to the court at Brimladin Ula."

Gage read the card aloud, then his head jerked up. "An honor, my lady."

Nara nodded but moved to the hearth and sat in one of the high-backed chairs before it. She waved the two men closer. "How long a journey would it be, general?"

"A week, possibly more," Gage said. "The roads have not been greatly maintained between our two countries."

"I had decided to accept the invitation, but now ... do you think it is wise for me to leave the territory now?

Gage frowned. "Perhaps it could be postponed?" Nara shook her head. "The occasion is the birhday and coming out of the young princess. There is not likely to be another such occasion soon, to warrant another invitation."

Burke sighed. "Adlair's letter is somewhat cryptic, but he seems to be hinting that there could be trouble, now that there is a queen in the Valley of Lhin."

Nara nodded. "I agree but I know Prince Eghan would never move against us in any way."

Gage handed her the letter. "If he is in control. But we do not know the intentions of this new queen, nor her father. Adlair seems to insinuate that they have exerted a negative influence over the king. If that is true, Eghan may not be able to prevent the trouble Adlair fears."

Nara stared at the general for a moment, a sense of dread flooding through her. She shook herself. "I think it is important to accept this invitation. I do not wish to insult a potentially friendly neighbor on our northern borders." She glanced at the letter again. "But perhaps you are right to be concerned. I do want to know our southern borders are secure before I leave."

Gage nodded. "I will put our army on alert there and renew our efforts to arm them more completely."

Nara nodded. "Spare no efforts in that regard, Gage, but ensure that the housing projects also go forward."

"I will see that it is done, my queen." Gage bowed and started to take his leave.

Nara stopped him. "I remember my father speaking highly of the King of the Brimleish, but he is now dead and gone. It is his son's signature on this invitation. Do you know of him?"

"Not much, I am afraid, but I will make inquiries immediately if you wish."

"Yes, do so. I would like to know as much as possible about him, his family and his people before I visit their court."

Nara watched Gage's face as he nodded. "The timing of this visit could be very advantageous, my lady. If we are able to secure a solid alliance with the Brimleish it could deter any army from coming against us. I have heard that the Brimleish forces are well trained and their seaports bustle with trade from far and wide."

Nara stood and paced to the window. "Yes. Perhaps an agreement could be reached. And we desperately need the trade."

Gage cleared his throat and when Nara turned to him his eyes twinkled. "One thing I have heard, my lady, the king and his brothers are quite handsome."

Nara turned away again so he could not see the sadness in her eyes. "This is a state visit only, general, and I would attend only for political reasons." She waved her hand. "Bring me a report as soon as possible. I should respond promptly."

Gage gave a small bow. "Of course, my lady." He nodded at Burke and took his leave.

Burke stepped closer. "I am at your disposal, my lady, if you wish to talk more."

Nara took his hand. "I am so thankful for your friendship and your loyalty, my friend."

Burke smiled, then glanced at the letter in her hand. "I will send a message to Adlair at once to let him know we received his letter safely. Do you wish to send something to Prince Eghan?"

Nara shook her head. "No... yes ... I ..." She began to say something else but choked on the words. Burke put his hand on her shoulder. Nara took a deep breath. "It's alright, Burke." She shook herself and stood. "I knew this day would come. Please convey my congratulations to the prince and his new bride."

Nara watched him go, then sat by the hearth, Adlair's letter dangling in her hand. Yes, she had known this day would come but she had hoped it would not. She had hoped ... she sighed and read the letter again.

"I know this will bring you pain, and for that I am deeply distressed, but the events that have so quickly unfolded here distress me even more ..."

Adlair did not go into great detail and she wondered what more he could have said and why he did not share it. Perhaps to spare her feelings, perhaps because he was conflicted about his own. Or perhaps he was afraid the letter might fall into the wrong hands.

Nara sighed again. Whatever the reason, Gage was right. If Adlair was worried they should be as well. She would make sure there was no sign of danger on her borders before leaving for Brimladin Ula.

Chapter Nineteen

Damon stood in a niche at the side of the king's great hall, watching. The people showed great respect for Gherin and he noted how the king deferred to his advisors and even his son. But he also noted that the king's face changed when Adlair spoke to Eghan. He noticed how his mouth twitched when the wizard touched the prince. The change was subtle but it was there. A fact that could be exploited. As the court dismissed, Damon smiled and stepped toward the dais. He bowed as the king acknowledged him.

"I have heard you enjoy a good game of chess, Your Majesty. I too find it satisfying and I must admit I fancy myself somewhat of an expert. I am always on the hunt for a worthy match. Would you be willing to engage in a game?"

Gherin nodded. "Of course. After the noon meal, perhaps?"

Damon bowed. "I would be honored, Your Majesty."

The game had just begun when Damon glanced at Silhas and Adlair, watching from the side of the chamber. He lowered his voice so only the king could hear. "I find the animosity of your advisors distracting, Your Majesty. We would have a more honest match without their hawk eyes staring at me."

Gherin looked up and waved his hand at the two men. As they slowly made their exit the king leaned toward Damon. "I apologize if they have shown any disrespect, Damon."

The Duke shrugged. "I understand their reticence, Your Majesty. I hope to gain their trust and even loyalty, in the days ahead." He smiled. "And your confidence as well."

The king dropped his head and focused on the board. They played in silence for some time, Damon allowing the king to best him but not without a show of skill. When Damon's king was knocked over Gherin lifted his chin and smiled. Damon stood and bowed. "Well played, Sire. I can see I have finally found a worthy opponent. Again, tomorrow?"

The king nodded. "I would be happy to best you again, Lord Damon."

Damon laughed, bowed, and left the room. He strode past Silhas and Adlair who stopped talking as he approached. He gave them a curt nod and a knowing smirk. He almost laughed aloud at the scowl on Silhas' face. *Soon I will be rid of you both,* he thought. *Yes, soon enough.*

Damon arranged that they meet for the chess games regularly and he was careful to let the king win just enough to keep him cocky and wanting to continue. They had finished a game that had lasted three days when Damon suggested a change in diversion.

"Although I have been enjoying our matches immensely, I am feeling the lack of physical exercise, Gherin." He smiled as he noted the king did not seem to object to being addressed by his proper name. "I wonder, do you ride out into your valley often?"

Gherin shook his head. "No, not often, Lord Damon," he said, "but if you wish, we could arrange it."

"A hunt, perhaps?" Damon suggested.

"A hunt! Yes, that would be excellent." The king smiled. I am sure Eghan would love to accompany us."

"Wonderful. It will give me a chance to get to know him a bit more. I fear he has been deliberately avoiding me. And Malora would love it as well. She is quite skilled with a bow."

"Of that I have no doubt," Gherin said.

Damon dropped his eyes for a moment in feigned humility. "Your Majesty," he said, then hesitated.

"Yes?" The king cocked his head and frowned.

"I know the circumstances of Malora and Eghan's match have not been the best, but the wedding has sealed the relationship between our families and our realms. I do hope it will grow to be an amicable alliance, in spite of its difficult beginning."

Gherin's eyes softened. "I am pleased to hear you speak this way, Lord Damon. I too would hope and pray for the same result."

Damon smiled and bowed low.

****

Malora breathed in the cool morning air as the horses stamped in the courtyard. A hunt was just what she wanted. She had been gracious with Eghan this morning, giving him her most winning smile and charming laughter at their breakfast. He did not seem to be quite as taken with it as he had been, but she noted a gleam of hopefulness in his eyes that almost made her smile genuine. She sighed. He was such a naive fool. She tried to push away the gnawing guilt but she was not entirely successful. Eghan's gentle nature and the king's genuine concern for her was wearing her down. She would have to guard herself against it. Her father would not tolerate such weakness.

She mounted her horse and caught the look in her father's eyes as he trotted alongside her. Their plans were advancing so well it was hard not to be cocky but he had warned her of being overly confident. Malora watched King Gherin mount and turned her head away for fear he would see the conflict in her eyes. She sighed at this other weakness that had shown itself in the past weeks. She was becoming truly fond of the old man. His concern for her had not wavered even after her subterfuge. That had confused her at first, but she was inclined to simply bask in it. She had never known such fatherly affection. She stiffened her back. No. She must not give in to such feelings. But the very knowledge that she could not, deepened her sadness.

As they rode out into the countryside Malora's mind swirled with these conflicting thoughts. She knew this day would mark a turning point for them all. Gherin Lhin was no match for her father's cunning, no matter what advisors and wizards he gathered around him. The trap about to unfold was perfect. The man's reign would soon be over and then she and her father would be free to take control.

Malora knew she should be thrilled that victory was so close but she felt only an emptiness that would not dissipate. If only things could be different. If only she could be rid of the fear that always gripped her when her father was nearby. If only Eghan .... she stopped herself from following that path of fantasy. Her destiny was set as surely as the Lhinian king's. There was nothing she could do, but obey her father and secure her own position in the world.

Eghan arrived and rode alongside her as the entourage moved out of the courtyard. She gave him a quick smile then kicked her horse and charged ahead of him. He followed at a close distance until she reined in her horse and fell back with the rest of the group.

They arrived at the edge of the woods and

dismounted. They would hunt in pairs. Malora was about to move into the bush with Eghan but her father's voice stopped her. "I hope you will not mind if I hunt with my daughter today, Prince Eghan," he said. "It may be the last opportunity I will have for some time."

Eghan glanced at her but dropped his eyes before recognizing the pleading look she gave him. He gave a short bow to Damon and moved away. Her father stepped closer. "Remember to cause the diversion after we stop for the meal," he said in a hushed voice. "Play the helpless woman well my dear."

She gave him a quick nod but said nothing. It took all of her training to push away her thoughts and focus on the hunt. They had stocked a small group of deer and had bagged three of them, one at her own hand, when the king called a halt. He directed the group to a grassy meadow by a small creek and ordered that the food be laid out. Malora could not help but be pleased when Eghan approached and helped her dismount.

"Are you well, Malora?" he asked, peering into her face. "You seem ... distracted."

Malora turned away. "I am just a bit weary, husband." She saw her father watching, turned and smiled at Eghan, then dropped her eyes at the puzzled and wary look in his. She tried to join in the light conversation as they ate, but was not very successful. When they began to gather to resume the hunt Malora positioned herself near the king. When she was sure he was turned toward her she gave a small moan and fell to the ground. She felt Gherin's arm under her shoulders and his hand on her cheek as he called her name. She kept her eyes closed until something cold was laid on her forehead. She blinked, feigning confusion. "Oh," she said. "What happened?"

"You collapsed." She knew King Gherin and Eghan were genuinely concerned as they peered down at her. She gave her head a bit of a shake. "Well, I am alright now, I'm sure." She began to sit up but Gherin put his hand on her arm. "Rest here for a moment, Malora. We will head back to the castle immediately."

Malora smiled at him. "No need, Your Majesty. Let the men continue their hunt. I am sure I will be just fine in a few moments."

Eghan called for a servant to bring a blanket and bent down to raise her head as he placed something soft under it. "We will hunt another day," he said. "We should get you back to the castle where a physician can attend to you, Malora."

Malora could not meet his eyes. She turned her head and found herself looking into her father's eyes instead. He gave her a satisfied smile that told her the diversion had given Rian sufficient time and opportunity to insert the burr beneath the king's saddle. She caught her father's look and put her hand on Gherin's arm. "Please, Your Majesty, it would upset me to know I have spoiled the day."

She gave Eghan a pleading look. "Please, do continue."

Her father nodded to the prince. "I will stay with Malora, Eghan. Continue your hunt as she has suggested. If I feel she is not well enough to ride in a short while I will send for a carriage to take her back."

The king nodded as Eghan stood. "Very well. We will not be much longer." He gave the order and the servants scrambled to obey.

Malora lay back and closed her eyes until the sound of the horses faded away. She heard her father chuckle and opened her eyes again.

"Well done, my dear."

She rolled onto her side and said nothing. It was not long before a servant charged back toward them. He stopped only briefly to tell them the king had fallen from his horse and a carriage would arrive as quickly as possible to take them both back to the castle.

Malora fumed at having to remain in her chamber for a few days. "We must make a good show of it," her father had said. She remembered his smile when he told her the king's physician had "suddenly become ill himself, poor fellow," so their own had been gratefully accepted as a substitute.

It was only a day or two before the king was steady on his feet again and able to attend to his duties. Damon's eyes gleamed with malevolence when he said, "he complains of the headaches, attributed to the fall of course, but is stoically soldiering on." He laughed out loud. "We are close, my dear, very close."

****

As the weeks went by after the accident, Eghan and the king's advisors became more and more uneasy. Eghan knew Silhas repeatedly cautioned Gherin but his words fell on deaf ears. The king spent many hours with Malora's father and his suspicion of him had turned to trust. Eghan became alarmed when his father consistently failed to meet with him for prayer, sending messages saying he was not feeling well or that he was "with our esteemed guests." Eghan took his concern to his uncle Adlair.

"It fills me with dread, Uncle." He groaned. "If only I had listened when you tried to warn me. I fell under Malora's spell. Now it appears my father has fallen under Damon's."

Adlair agreed. "He refuses to listen to any council against the man and the continuing headaches are a concern as well. We must do what we can on our own to find out what Damon and his daughter are plotting. Tell the servants to keep their ears and eyes open, Eghan. Speak to Malora. I do not expect she will divulge anything willingly, but she might let something slip. I will tell Khalwyd to report anything suspicious immediately."

It did not take long before suspicious things were noticed. Khalwyd called them together and told them he was shocked to see Damon's soldiers joining Gherin's at their posts. A captain of the guard had looked puzzled when Khalwyd questioned him about it. "He said it is by the king's order. Each soldier is to have one of Lord Damon's men at his side. I have tried to object -- the men are uneasy about it, to say the least, but the King is easily angered these days." He lowered his voice a notch. "Did you know he has threatened to imprison members of his own guard for being disrespectful toward this Duke Damon and his lot?"

Eghan shook his head. "No, I did not know that. And it appears there are many things that are being kept hidden."

"Keep us informed, Khalwyd," Adlair said. "I do not like what is happening any more than you."

As the weeks lengthened into months, Adlair and Khalwyd became more and more fearful. Finally, they went before the king. Eghan stood with them as they approached and expressed their concern.

Khalwyd's eyes were narrowed. "Every day more of them come inside the town, Sire, and every night fewer of them leave. I am certain more soldiers have arrived to occupy the tents of those who are now inside our walls."

Gherin waved his hand as though to dismiss him. "Damon's people have a right to move freely among us, Khalwyd. Our families have been joined."

Adlair spoke strongly. "They are not to be trusted,

Gherin. Surely you see how we are putting ourselves in great jeopardy by..."

The king raised his hand and interrupted. "Our initial instincts were wrong. Duke Damon is very wise. I am sure he has no ill intent. He has been gracious, considering the circumstances of his daughter's betrothal." Eghan dropped his eyes when his father's glance fell on him. "We have both agreed to make the best of it, to make ours a beneficial alliance."

Khalwyd's frown deepened. "I still do not trust him sire, nor his scheming daughter."

Eghan stiffened as the king's voice rose. "Malora is now my daughter, Khalwyd. Be careful how you speak of her." When Khalwyd bowed his head, Gherin spoke in a more normal tone. "Her actions were somewhat unseemly, I agree, but, well, the girl was in love. You know how women can be when they are after something. It will all work out to our advantage. Damon and I are making plans that will be of great benefit."

Adlair's eyebrows shot up. "Plans? What kind of plans? And of benefit to whom?"

The king's gaze was cold as he answered. "To all those who are loyal and faithful to me, brother."

Eghan caught the sarcastic tone of the last word and a chill ran up his spine. The king dismissed them, refusing to discuss anything more.

Chapter Twenty

Damon stepped from behind a heavy curtain, where he had watched as the king dismissed his advisor curtly. He smiled at the king. "You are handling this situation well, my friend."

Gherin frowned. "Are you sure your suspicions about Adlair and Silhas can be proven, Damon?"

"Your own servants have told us how the wizard and your advisor have schemed against you, Gherin. They intend to be rid of you as soon as possible, thinking that when Eghan is king they will gain more control. That was the true intent of the abduction, to befriend the boy, gain his trust and eventually turn him against you. Think, Sire, you have seen how they conspire to keep Eghan away from you. Keeping him caught up in that building, for instance, and taking him out among the people where he is so vulnerable. Does that sound like protection?"

"But I cannot believe they would ..."

"Shall I send for the servants again, so they can testify..."

Gherin rubbed at his temples "No. I have no

stomach to hear it again."

Damon put a hand on the king's shoulder. "I hesitate to speak of this now, my friend, but...

The king raised his head. "What? Who has turned against me now?"

"I fear Khalwyd is in league with them, Sire."

Gherin shook his head. "No. Impossible. Khalwyd has guarded Eghan all his life. He would never do anything to bring harm to the House of Lhin. He has always had my family's best interests at heart."

"Exactly. The man has been deluded into believing it will be best for the boy if you are removed. The wizard is behind it all, Gherin. You must be rid of him."

Gherin moaned and put a hand to his head again. "I should never have allowed him to return."

Damon lowered his voice and leaned toward the king. "His arrival was the beginning of it all. Interesting, is it not, that this prophet you spoke of proclaimed his message of doom just prior to the wizard's arrival? Was it not he who seduced you into believing such a thing could be true? I know it must be hard to learn of such treachery, Gherin, but be glad you have Malora and I to stand with you. Believe me, we will not allow power to fall into the wrong hands. You should thank your God we arrived in time."

Gherin did not answer. A nagging voice in his mind reminded him again that it had been weeks since he had prayed, weeks since he had thanked his God for anything. He sighed deeply. The pounding in his head made his head swim. "I have to think about these things, Damon. Please leave me now."

"Shall I send for my physician, Sire?"

"Yes," Gherin nodded.

Damon bowed slightly and left the king alone.

Gherin sat for some time, letting the physician's potions work. It was odd the way some of them seemed to work so well but others only made the pain worse. He would talk with him about it soon. But then he realized he could not remember what the man had given him. Which drug made the pain worse and which one made it better? He shook his head, then stood slowly and walked from the room, trying to clear his mind. He felt so weary. So very weary.

He was so distracted he did not hear the sound of a young woman crying as he made his way along the corridor. If she had not collided with him, he would not have noticed her.

Malora's tear-stained face registered with shock and confusion as the king grasped her arms to keep her from sagging to the floor.

"Oh ...oh, Your Majesty, forgive me. I....I..." She glanced over her shoulder.

"What is it, child? You look terrified."

The girl burst into a renewed flood of tears. Gherin took her arm gently and led her into the great hall, yelling for a servant to bring water. He seated her and continued to pat her hand until she was able to gain control. She tried to apologize again.

"I am so sorry, Sire."

"Hush, Malora. Tell me what has upset you."

Malora buried her head in her hands. "Oh, my Lord, I do not want to cause you pain."

Gherin drew the girl's hands down and lifted her chin. "Tell me."

"It ... it was Adlair, my Lord. He said such awful things to me." She lowered her eyes and forced a flush to her face. "I ... I cannot even repeat ..."

Gherin's voice was low. "How dare he..."

Malora looked into his face with a pleading expression. "Oh, please, Sire, do not tell him I told you. He threatened ..."

"He dared threaten you? I'll have the man flogged!"

"No, Sire, please. I ... I am so afraid of what he might do. He said he would use his powers to..."

"You have nothing to fear from him, Malora." Gherin put his arm around the girl. "He will not be a danger to you or to anyone else. I will see to that." He raised her from the chair. "Now come, I will send for your maids to attend you."

"You have been so good to me, Sire. I ... I ... do not deserve your kindness."

"Hush, child. Go and rest, now, and do not worry. I will deal with the wizard."

****

Eghan and Khalwyd had just finished a round of mock battle in the outer courtyard. Eghan wiped his brow with his forearm. They had been rigorous about the training lately and Eghan was aware that Khalwyd was more earnest than ever about it. As they stopped to rest he noticed Khalwyd did not sheath his sword but let it rest loosely in his hand. When Latham burst in, the guardian instinctively tightened his grip on the weapon. The boy rushed at them, talking from the moment he saw Eghan, until he grasped the boy's shoulders and tried to get him to slow down.

Latham peered earnestly up at him. "You must help, m'lord! The king has sent his own guards!" The boy grasped Eghan's hand and tried to pull him away.

Khalwyd frowned down at him. "What are you babbling about, boy?"

Eghan spoke quickly. "Explain yourself, Latham."

The page tugged on his arm again. "I don't know what she told him, m'lords, but the king is furious. The servants say he's threatened to have him flogged. You must help!"

"Flogged? Who is he having flogged? Let go of me, Latham!"

In desperation, the page released the prince's arm and stamped his foot. "Please, sir, there isn't much time."

The hair on the back of Eghan's neck suddenly stood on end. He grasped Latham's shoulders again and shook him. "Latham, you are not making any sense. Who are you talking about?"

"Your uncle, m'Lord, the Lord Adlair. He's been arrested."

"Arrested? For what reason?"

"They say Malora has accused him, m'Lord, but of what I don't know. I only know the king is furious."

Khalwyd and Eghan exchanged glances and all three hurried into the castle.

The king was hunched into a chair in the great hall, Damon hovering at his side. Eghan noted the cold look on his father's face, the lines of pain around his eyes.

"Father, what..."

Gherin raised his hand to interrupt him. "He has gone too far, Eghan, and shown his true colors at last. We can no longer deny it. The man is dangerous to us all."

"Dangerous? Father, how can you..."

"I will not discuss it!"

Eghan felt as though he had been physically struck.

Khalwyd stepped forward. "But you must discuss it Sire. There obviously has been some confusion ..."

Damon straightened. "The king has taken action to prevent further embarrassment to the House of Lhin. Be grateful."

It was all Eghan could do to keep himself from leaping on the man. His glare spoke for itself. "And what have you had to do with this, Damon Gille?"

Gherin stood to his feet. "I will not allow you to

speak to your father-in-law, our guest, in that tone, Eghan."

Eghan approached him. "Father, Uncle Adlair would never do anything to harm Malora. Her accusations must be false."

"You dare suggest my daughter is lying?" Damon took a step forward.

"I suggest there is a mistake," Eghan answered without turning. "How it came to be, I do not know."

"There is no mistake, Eghan." Damon's voice turned soft, enticing. "You have been deceived, son. It is time to see the truth." He placed a hand on Eghan's shoulder.

"I am not your son." Eghan almost spat the words as he whirled around, shook his head and took a step backwards, repelled by the evil flowing out of the man.

The king grasped Eghan's arm. "It is true, Eghan. Adlair has conspired for years to remove me from the throne. I believe he has won your trust only for that reason. I suspect the wizard may even have cast a spell on you. He means only to bring harm to us all, including you, and your bride."

Eghan pulled free. "No. It is you who has been deceived, Father, by this ... this man, if he is in fact human."

Gherin's face reddened and his voice filled the room. "Leave us! Leave us now, before I do something I will regret."

Eghan's hand went to his sword and he began to

turn toward Malora's father but Khalwyd put a hand on his arm.

The king moved between them. His voice was low and cold. "I command you to leave us!"

Eghan stared into his father's face. All the days of closeness were wiped away. The cold hard barrier was between them again, as though it had never been removed. When he felt Khalwyd's grip on his arm tighten he was relieved to give in to it, to turn away from his father's face.

Once in the corridor, Eghan sank against the wall, his hands clenched at his sides. "What can we do, Khal," he moaned. "What can we do?"

"We must free Adlair. Whatever it takes, we must get him away. Damon will not stop until your uncle is rendered powerless but perhaps he will drop his guard once Adlair is gone." Khalwyd's voice was level but deep with the same sadness Eghan felt. "Then we will try again to reason with your father." He gripped Eghan's shoulder and pulled him away from the wall. "Come. We must plan how to do it."

****

Eghan peered out over the walls of his father's castle. The evening was calm, a trace of winter in the air. But his thoughts were anything but calm. Emotions whirled inside him. Anger, love, hatred. They seemed to blend into one. He leaned heavily on the stone casement and groaned. "Lord, show me what to do. I do not know even what to feel."

A small scraping noise made him whirl around. Malora stood watching him. Eghan thought he caught a glint of sadness in her face, but his words were cutting.

"Come to gloat, Malora?"

She shook her head. "You ... you haven't spoken to me for days."

"I have nothing to say to you."

She took a step toward him. "Eghan..."

"Do not come any closer."

She looked like he had struck her. He regretted his harsh tone, but said nothing more.

"We are married."

"A legality only, as you yourself have insisted." The bitter words hung in the air.

She dropped her head, then raised her eyes to him. "There could be more, so much more if..."

"If what, Malora? If I join your father and betray my own?" He saw the glint in her eyes. "That is what you and your father are planning, is it not? To gain control?" He took a step toward her. "Is it not?"

Suddenly Malora was in his arms, her beautiful face looking up into his, a longing there Eghan had not seen before.

"We could have each other, Eghan. That is all I want now."

Eghan's pulse throbbed in his head. His mind whirled with opposite possibilities. One voice seemed to scream, "You can have it all, Eghan, the world at your feet, a beautiful woman at your side.

Just say yes to her now." The other voice broke through. "The cost is too high, Eghan. Refuse her. Turn away from her. Now."

As though Malora sensed his confusion she reached up and touched his face. "We would be in control, Eghan. You and I. Join me. We could have it all, a wonderful life here together. My father will soon have control of Alinga Territory once again. Once we have the ore from Alingan mines we would be unconquerable, Eghan, invincible. We could..."

Eghan's mind raced. Once again... ? He pushed her away and caught his breath as her words seared his mind. Control of the Alinga Territory once again ... the realization struck. "Your father was in league with Malnar. He fought with him to deny Nara her throne." He grasped Malora's arms. "Didn't he?"

The girl's face hardened. She raised her chin. "My father is more powerful than that wretched Duke Malnar ever was. If my father had been in control of the Alingans, we would not have lost that battle. We would have secured power and we would have come against you in force." She smiled, and Eghan saw the greed and hatred fill her eyes. "You can be assured, my prince, we will take control of this valley, then we will take control of Alinga Territory again and put an end to that wench who stole it from us. We will ..."

Eghan dropped his hands and whispered Nara's name.

Malora's face contorted with jealousy. Her hands clenched and released as she moved away from him. She stamped her foot like a petulant child.

"Fool! You will lose this time, Eghan Lhin. You and that Nara, both. You will lose everything!" She whirled around and fled.

Chapter Twenty-one

It was Silhas who formed the plan. They would take the offensive. Khalwyd would distract Damon's men while Eghan confronted the guards and demanded the release of his uncle. As they hurried toward the cells, Eghan prayed the guards would respond to his authority as their prince. As he prayed his heart beat hard. Princes had been accused of treason for less than what he was about to do. At the entrance to the prison he was relieved to see Silhas greet an old friend.

Jhonar's smile was brief. "I have been expecting you, Silhas."

"We have come to see Lord Adlair."

"An ambassador in chains."

"Once again."

Jhonar's eyes darted to Damon's men.

"Circumstances are different, my friend."

"But the Lord is with us."

Jhonar nodded and opened the first door. As they stepped through, he leaned close and said softly, "I'll keep these ones away from the door as long as I can. Be quick."

There were not many guards in the corridors until they reached the level where Adlair was held. Khalwyd slipped away and hid himself. As Eghan and Silhas walked boldly toward Adlair's cell, Eghan noticed there were two of Damon's men for every Lhinian.

Silhas spoke first. "We have come to see the prisoner. Open the door."

Two of the king's men exchanged a look. Damon's men took a step forward but before they could respond, Eghan spoke with authority.

"By the authority of the king, open it now!"

One of the Lhinian guards produced a key and swiftly unlocked the cell. As they moved toward it, Eghan heard Khalwyd's yell. It was enough to distract the men for a moment and that was all they needed. Adlair was out and running with them in a matter of seconds.

Eghan glanced over his shoulder as they fled and saw his father's soldiers holding Damon's men at bay. They made the upper entrance easily. As they leaped into the open, Eghan's heart beat with victory, but it was short-lived. They had taken only a few steps when they were surrounded by Damon's men, swords drawn. Eghan saw Khalwyd start to raise his weapon, but Adlair put a restraining hand on his arm. Resistance was futile against so many. Eghan clenched his fists in frustration. They had stepped right into a trap. The circle of soldiers parted and Damon himself was before them, smiling. He eyed each of them. His smile was smug.

"Well, well. Treason against the king by his closest advisors." He smirked as he faced Eghan. "And even his own son."

Eghan wanted to drive his fist into the glinting white teeth, but he was helpless as the guards separated him from the others and herded them all toward the great hall.

The room was crowded when they burst in, the guards dragging Khalwyd, who had attempted to break free and still wrestled with his captors. Gherin stood in silence as Damon loudly presented the charge of treason against Adlair, Silhas and Khalwyd. As he spoke, he slowly made his way toward the king, until he stood on the dais beside him.

"You can deny the truth no longer, King Gherin. The proof stands before you. Even your own son has..."

"Silence!"

The king turned on the duke and Eghan's heart leaped. For a moment he thought his father had seen through the deception. But Gherin spoke coldly when he turned back to the three men on their knees before him.

"I have trusted you with my life, and the life of my son. You have repaid me with treachery and betrayal."

Khalwyd lunged to his feet. "Sire, by all that is holy and good, I swear we meant no challenge to the rule of your kingdom, nor harm to you, nor to your son. We were only trying to thwart the plan of a devious enemy - a snake, who has slithered in and brought evil among us."

Damon stepped closer to the king. "The witnesses you have already heard will swear again that these men have conspired against you, Gherin. Secure your throne. Stop this treachery before it destroys what you have built."

Gherin paused for only a moment. He seemed to sway slightly and his hand went to his head. Then he shook himself and stared down at the three men. "All of you will hang."

Eghan surged forward. "No!"

Damon's guards were on him, pinning his arms.

Khalwyd took a step forward, his voice a bellow. "I have served you all my life. I ..."

Before he could finish, a guard struck him with the butt end of a long lance. Khalwyd crumpled to the ground.

Eghan writhed in the arms of his captors. "Father, please, you cannot do this. You have been poisoned by this ... Damon. You must know in your heart we are not against you."

Damon leaned toward the king briefly and spoke too softly for anyone to hear. Gherin faced them and his look made Eghan's heart stop. His father's gaze fell again on the three kneeling at his feet. He waved his hand over them, as though over a pile of dung, and spoke to the guards. "Take them away."

Eghan struggled again, but could not break free of the tight grip of Damon's men. The Duke leaned toward the king once more and Gherin's eyes turned on his son. The anger faded, but what Eghan saw there wounded him more deeply than anything ever had. For the first time in his life, he saw the look of defeat in his father's eyes.

The king stared for a moment, his eyes seeming to glaze over, then he gave a slight jerk of his head. Damon nodded and stepped away from him. With a wave of his hand and the command, "Follow me," he led them out of the great hall.

Once they were away from the king, Damon ordered Eghan to be bound. Then he deliberately led them out through the courtyard and into the open square. In no time a crowd gathered, forcing the guards to make a path for them as they marched toward the house of prayer.

At its entrance, Damon turned and smirked into Eghan's face. "Fitting, is it not, Prince Eghan, that you will be held here? Your prison will be the very house on which you have labored." Then he turned to the people still swarming about them and raised his voice. "Spread the word. Prince Eghan's attempt to overthrow his father's rule has been thwarted. His treasonous friends will hang and he will be held in isolation until we are convinced he has come to his senses and is free of the wizard's spell." He nodded at the guards and Eghan was pushed through the high wooden doors.

Eghan watched over his shoulder as Damon stood

at the entrance, surveying the crowd for a few moments. Then he turned, smiled, and bolted the huge doors behind him.

Eghan struggled again but could not free himself. He felt as helpless as a child as he was dragged across the sanctuary toward the small door leading to the high room above them that had been intended for secluded prayer. Eghan knew once he was locked in that room there was no escape.

Chapter Twenty-two

Malora sat still, peering into space, her face expressionless, her back stiff with tension. Her father sat calmly while his brother paced.

"We must force the prince to cooperate, Damon," Rian said. "When his people see him by Malora's side, they will not resist. Without him, we risk a costly rebellion. You must..."

"I must do no-one's bidding but my own." Damon had not raised his voice, but the tone sent a shiver up Malora's back and made Rian take a step back.

"Of course, of course, I was only suggesting..."

"Your suggestions have been noted. The boy will be made ready to join us, in time. What of the other plans?"

"The poison has been doing its work. One more dose and it will be over. A small vial poured into his evening wine, and he dies in his sleep."

Malora wanted to run from the room. Bile rose in her throat and she feared she would vomit. She gripped the arms of her chair and remained silent.

Damon's voice was cold. "It must be well timed. The prince will be within my power in a few days.

He must return to the castle immediately after the king's death, to assume power with his queen. Then, after a time, you may arrange one of your unfortunate accidents."

Rian nodded. "I have thought it through. An accident while riding with his new bride, a fall, witnessed only by his grieving young widow." He smiled at Malora. "Of course she will be distraught, but determined to do what is best for the people. It will have them all eating from her hands."

Malora whirled on him. "And what of the next step?"

Her uncle smiled. "Do you think we have not planned the final stage, Malora, the purpose for all of this?"

"I think you had better ensure its success, Uncle, or your head may be the price to be paid."

"How dare you threaten me..."

Damon stood and in one long stride was between them. "Malora is my daughter, Rian. Answer her!"

The man's eyes dropped. His voice was flat as he spoke. "Messengers have been paid to arrive soon after the prince's death, with news of the Alingans massing at the border."

"Excellent." Damon turned and eyed Malora. "These Lhinians are fools. They will fight to preserve what they have already lost and in doing so secure our future."

Malora did not meet her father's eyes.

****

Damon peered down at the man slouched on the throne. A smirk began to form at his mouth, but he changed the expression quickly as the king looked up.

"I cannot do it, Damon."

"You must, Your Majesty. To show weakness now would be foolish. No doubt there are others waiting to seize control at any sign of failure to act. You must hang them, and quickly."

The King turned away and sank deeper into the throne. He pressed his hands to his temples. His voice almost trembled when he asked, "Has Eghan admitted the treachery?"

"Not yet, and that is all the more reason to hang the wizard and his cohorts. We must break their power over the prince. Once they are gone, the boy will see clearly how he was deceived."

"I want to see him. If I speak with him I am sure ..."

Damon put a hand on the king's shoulder. "It is best to keep him isolated for a time, my friend. He is being well cared for. I am seeing to that personally. I know this is difficult for you, but it is for Eghan's good and yours. We must ensure he returns to reason as soon as possible, for his own good and the good of your realm."

Gherin raised his head. "I was hoping there would be new evidence, something to prove it has all been a mistake."

Damon squeezed the king's shoulder. "Treachery has always been a part of history, Gherin. Only

those who guard against it and act swiftly, survive."
****

Eghan woke shivering on a cold stone floor. The room was dark, barely a glimmer of light seeping through cracks in the wooden roof. He tried to think how long he had been there. Was it a day? Two days? He shook himself and sat up. No-one had come to see him since Damon's men dragged him here. He had been given no food nor water. Did they mean to let him die this way? Would his father allow it? Did his father even know what was happening to him?

The look that had been in the king's eyes tortured Eghan worse than his hunger and thirst. The thought that his friends were to be executed nearly drove him mad. Were they already dead? He stood to his feet and beat against the heavy door. The sound barely echoed in his prison chamber. He knew no-one would hear it. He was helpless and utterly alone. He slid to his knees and put his head in his hands.

"God, why have you done this?"

"Trust me."

Eghan pushed himself to his feet, peering into the darkness. The voice had seemed to boom from the stone. Hope surged through him. Then he heard footsteps, the sound of heavy boots ascending the stairs. He listened intently as the sound came closer. He heard the beam scrape across the other side of the door, then a lantern was thrust toward him and rough hands grabbed his arms, binding them tightly behind him. A strip of leather was pushed over his head and pulled tight around Eghan's throat. A rough voice said in his ear, "Attempt to free yerself and I'll strangle ye." The leather tightened. "Understand?"

He nodded and was shoved forward, down the narrow stairway and into the main hall of the House of Prayer. He peered into the dimness for several moments before realizing a man sat in a throne-like chair at the far end of the room. Eghan was shoved forward again, then forced to his knees before Damon Gille.

Damon smiled. "You do not look well, Prince Eghan. Perhaps some water will help?" He gave a flick of his wrist.

A servant approached with a dipper and held it before Eghan's face. When Damon nodded, he held it to Eghan's lips only long enough for one gulp, then dropped it, sending a stream of water across the floor. It took all of Eghan's will power to keep from flinging himself down to lick the life-giving liquid from the stone.

Damon's voice was thick with mock regret. "The boy is so clumsy. But I am sure you will forgive him, will you not?" He stood and towered over Eghan. "We will forgive you, Eghan, if you but admit you were under your uncle's perverse control. Testify that he poisoned your mind against your father and you can come back to your own soft bed, to your father's table, to your lovely wife.

Everything will be restored to you, Prince Eghan. Just tell the people your uncle and the others deserve to hang."

Eghan raised his head and looked into the eyes of his captor as he calmly replied, "Never."

Damon smirked down at him.

"They will hang, with or without your testimony. You cannot save them, but you can save yourself. You will not even have to speak. Just nod your head when asked the question, and you will be released."

"Never," Eghan repeated.

Damon's eyes narrowed. "We shall see."

By the next day, Eghan could think of nothing but his thirst. When they dragged him from the cell he prayed for the strength to stand. When Damon's servant again allowed him only a mouthful before spilling the water out before him, he almost wept. But he refused to betray his uncle and his friends. When they brought him out on the third day, there was a table set in the hall, covered with steaming food and large goblets of water and wine. Damon sat on his throne and smiled. The guards tied Eghan into a chair opposite him.

The man waved his hand at the table. "It all belongs to you, Eghan. Simply do as I ask and you will have it all."

Eghan tried not to look at the food, tried not to smell its aroma, tried not to think of the cool water sitting only inches away. He stared at Damon and remained silent.

When at last they returned him to his cold cell, he begged the guards to help him.

"Please. I need water. Please."

The guards laughed and pushed him roughly to the floor. Sneering down, one kicked him viciously. As the door was heaved shut and bolted, Eghan cringed against the wall and tried to pray.

When they returned for him the next day, he could not stand. If they had let go of him he would have tumbled down the stairway like a rag. He was barely aware they had stopped at a landing, nor did he care, until Damon's voice hissed in his ear.

"Look, Prince of the House of Lhin, witness your defeat."

The guards pushed him toward the window opening. Below them, on a high scaffold in a glowing morning sun, stood three men, their backs to the tower. Their heads hooded, their necks wrapped by thick ropes, they stood motionless on the gallows. Eghan's mind tried to register the meaning of what he was seeing. Who were these men, about to be executed before him? Damon leaned into the open window and raised his arm. The executioner tugged the hood from one man's head and a mass of red hair shone in the light. As the stocky man struggled, Eghan caught a glimpse of his face.

Eghan's eyes widened in horror and he screamed, "Khalwyd!" The name echoed back to them from the cold stone. Damon signaled again and the hood was swiftly pulled over the man's head before he could turn fully toward the sound. The nooses were tightened on all three. Each trap door gave a deep thud as it was released.

"No!" Eghan's screams roared in his own ears. "No!"

It took several moments for the hanging bodies to be still.

****

Nara sank to her knees before the window seat. The burden she felt almost crushed her. She gasped for air and called out, "God, help me!"

Brynna was at her side instantly. Nara grasped her hand as her handmaid helped her back into the window seat where a copy of The Book lay open.

"My lady?" Brynna's eyes were full of concern. "What is it?"

Nara shook her head. "I don't know, Brynna. I only know something terrible has happened. Eghan ..." She remembered the moment that seemed so long ago, when she knew her childhood nurse had been killed by Duke Malnar. She shook her head again. "No," she whispered. "No, not Eghan too. Please God, not Eghan."

Brynna knelt beside her. "We must pray, my lady."

Nara peered into her eyes. "I cannot form the words."

"Then I will pray for us both."

Nara nodded and bowed her head. As Brynna's words poured out, Nara felt a calmness begin to flood into her. She gathered it in as a thirsty deer takes in life-giving water. Then she too, prayed. When there were no more words in her, she stood.

"I must speak to Gage and Burke, Brynna. Immediately."

The girl curtsied and fled from the room.

Chapter Twenty-three

Eghan heard the bar scrape against the other side of the door. He closed his eyes and let his head sag back against the wall. What did Damon have in store for him now? He opened his eyes as the door opened and he heard the russle of a woman's dress. He pushed himself to his feet as Malora entered.

She wrapped her arms around his neck and when she lifted her face to his it was wet with tears.

"Please, Eghan, please, do as my father wishes. Your uncle is dead. There is no reason to resist now. Admit the wizard was manipulating you, then we can begin to build a life together."

Eghan pushed her away.

Malora's face changed. "My father will find other ways to torture you if you continue to refuse."

"I will not betray my friends, though they lie in a cold grave."

"Friends?" Malora scoffed. "They were only men who have always wanted something from you, Eghan. Don't be such a fool. You were their door to all they wanted - the power of honored places in your father's kingdom. You meant nothing more to them than a bit of silver that could buy the choicest cuts of meat."

Eghan turned his back to her. She was silent for a moment and he thought she would leave but then he felt her body press against his back.

"Do I mean nothing at all to you, Eghan?"

He turned, put his hands on her arms and pushed her back. "I offered you what I could give, Malora, and you refused it, betraying me and my father's trust. I know I am that piece of silver to you and nothing more. Whatever I felt for you once is dead."

Malora's eyes narrowed. "You will regret that, my prince. My father's torturers are skilled. It won't take them long to break you."

Eghan dropped his hands. "I willingly take whatever is to come. I will never betray my father. Nor will I allow your father to use me as a tool to deceive my people. I will never stand before them again with you as my queen."

Malora whirled around and left the chamber. Eghan slumped back against the cold stone as the door was once again locked and barred.

****

It took several moments for the sound to register in Eghan's mind. It was a scraping noise, too deliberate and consistent to be the scratching of an animal. He sat up and listened, then turned toward the sound. He placed his ear to the outside wall and listened again. The noise was coming from the other side. Eghan moved along the wall until he located the exact stone. It was about chest high and larger than the others. In the dimness, Eghan tried to examine it more carefully. He felt along its edge and discovered the mortar was not solid and the stone was slightly recessed. A surge of hope thrilled him as he placed both palms against it and pushed. The noise ceased. The stone had moved.

It took several more heaves and all of Eghan's strength for him to push the stone completely out. He heard the thump as its weight hit the ground far below. He began to raise himself to peer through the hole, then slumped back as a hand suddenly thrust itself toward him. A shaggy head appeared, then the small shoulders of a boy. He wormed his way through and tumbled into Eghan's cell.

"Oomph. Sorry, m'lord, did I scare ye?" The boy had almost landed on top of him.

Eghan couldn't believe his ears. "Latham?"

"Aye, m'lord, it's me, all right."

"But how..."

"T'was Master Ulhrik, sir, he dragged me by the ear, he did. No sense of humor, that old coot. Don't tell him I called him that, melord. Not that I didn't want to help, ye understand, but this tower is high, sir, and it's dark and ..."

"Latham, how did you get up here?"

"Notches, m'lord."

"Notches?"

"Yes, sir. That Ulhrik's a trickster, he is. Thought I was inside, I did, till I stepped on a stone and the wall moved. Scared me half to death, it did, t' find meself on the outside of the wall, an so far up! Wouldn't 'ave moved another mite, if Master Ulhrik hadn't poked me with that stick o' his." The lad twisted and pulled a wineskin from where it had hung down his back. "He thought maybe you'd be needin water, melord, so..."

Eghan grabbed the skin from the boy's hands and guzzled for several minutes, feeling his strength return as he did so. When he could drink no more, Eghan stood and peered through the open hole in the wall. It was too thick to see the outer edge. "Can we climb down, Latham, as easily as you came up?"

"Wouldn't say it was easy, m'lord, them notches is small and hard to see and..."

"Latham!"

The boy blinked before answering. "I expect that was Master Ulhrik's idea, if you can squeeze yerself through the hole, melord. There's a stone stickin' out, to the side of it, to grab onto. The notches start just below." Latham eyed his master. "But can ye manage it, m'lord. Ye looks a bit weak."

Eghan eyed the opening. "I'll manage, boy, I'll manage. Quickly then, you first."

Latham stuck his head into the opening, then withdrew it again. "Can't we wait till dawn, sir? It's a bit risky, tryin t' see them notches in the dark."

Eghan gave the boy a gentle shove. "Now, Latham, before someone decides to investigate the thud of that stone."

The boy sighed and slipped into the opening,

twisted his body sideways and disappeared. Eghan followed, finding the hole tight but passable. His legs slipped over the edge, then the rest of his body. He gripped the opening and felt to the side where Latham had said the notches started. At first there was nothing but solid, smooth stone and for a moment Eghan felt panic rising in his throat. A fall from this height would be certain death. Then his hand touched a protrusion. He gripped it and eased one leg out, feeling the stone until his toe slipped into a notch, not deep, but enough. Taking a breath of the cold night air, Eghan released his grip on the edge of the hole above and felt for something else to grip. It only took a few moments to find another groove in the stone. Slowly, he lowered himself down the side of the tower. The wind whipped at him as he descended and more than once his body's weakness made him tremble, but he kept moving.

Eghan was still a considerable way from the ground when his foot suddenly swung into open space. He gripped the notches and hugged the surface of the stone until he felt a hand grasp his ankle and draw his foot onto a narrow ledge, then he stepped down onto a wider one, then he was inside, standing in the dark on a solid landing. A hand gripped his arm as he heard Ulhrik's voice say in a whisper, "Hurry, this way." As they moved away, Eghan heard a slow grinding noise and knew the hole where he had just stood had once again become a solid wall. His knees turned to rubber, he stumbled and Ulhrik's old arms went round him, half carrying him down what seemed to be an unending descent.

When they finally stopped on another landing, Ulhrik left him leaning against a wall. Eghan's legs gave out entirely and he sank to the cold floor. Latham pressed the water skin to his lips and he drank, then struggled to his feet again. Just before the old man returned with a lit torch, Eghan felt a slight vibration in the stone. They had only gone another few paces when the floor beneath them seemed to drop from sight. Eghan pulled back until Ulhrik held the torch down, showing a steep descent, more like a ladder than a stairway. Latham was the first to turn his back to the hole and lower himself down. Eghan heard Ulhrik's voice again.

"Courage, Prince Eghan, we are almost there."

When he woke he could not remember descending the last few feet. He was stretched out on a pile of straw, a rough wool blanket covering him. He smiled ruefully to himself. Something about this felt familiar. He raised his head and looked around, half expecting to see Khalwyd stretched out near him. When he saw Latham, propped up against the wall, asleep, sadness flooded through him. Khalwyd would not be by his side ever again. He noticed Ulhrik standing at a small opening, staring out. When Eghan thought of the view from that window, the memory came surging back and he groaned.

Ulhrik turned to him, then went to his side as Eghan slouched back onto his bed. Ulhrik pulled bread and cheese from a sack as he spoke. "This must be enough for now, young prince. We have much to do and no time for a feast."

Eghan ate without tasting, then forced himself to his feet. His voice was without urgency when he spoke. "They will have discovered my absence by now, Ulhrik. We must get out of here."

The old man shook his head. "No. The house of prayer will be your refuge and fortress now, Prince Eghan. The battle will be won or lost from here."

"But..."

Ulhrik held up his hand. "Patience, boy, patience. The plan is already afoot."

Eghan's eyes opened wider. "What plan? Devised by whom?"

"By your uncle, of course, and Khalwyd and Silhas."

Eghan stared and for a moment words would not come out of his mouth. When they did they were almost a whisper. "But they are dead."

Ulhrik frowned at him. "They are as alive as I, unless I have been conversing with ghosts of late."

"But I saw ... three men were hanged ..." He moved to the window and peered down. The gallows stood, grey and solid as stone. "There, in the courtyard below. It was Khalwyd and ..."

Ulhrik was shaking his head. "They are alive, Eghan. The king has not yet given the order. His reluctance is to his credit. It seems Damon's poison has not completely taken hold. At least, not yet. Khalwyd and the others are safely ensconced in the dungeons at the moment, though from what I have heard, it is more like their private chambers than a prison. It seems the captain of the guard is a friend."

Eghan's relief made him light-headed for a moment. He sagged against the stone and peered down into the courtyard. Rousing himself, he rushed to Ulhrik and grabbed the old man's boney shoulders. "Tell me the plan, and quickly, Ulhrik. We are wasting time."

The old man smiled and patted Eghan's hand. With exaggerated effort, he squatted down on the straw at their feet and pulled a piece of bread from the sack. He tore a piece off and put it in his mouth, chewing as though he were tasting it for the first time.

Eghan groaned but knew better than to push him. His frustration obvious, he gave Latham a none too gentle nudge with his foot.

"Wake up, boy."

"Huh?" Latham scrubbed his eyes with his fists. "What is it, m'lord? Are we off again?"

"No. Just wake up."

"Why, m'lord?"

Ulhrik cackled. "Because your master is impatient, Latham, and his frustration demands that he take it out on someone. A rather ungentlemanly thing to do, wouldn't you say?"

Eghan paced the length of the small room twice, then squatted in front of the old prophet. "Tell me!"

Ulhrk's hooded eyes remained downcast for a few moments but when he raised them to meet Eghan's they were full of fire. "A good part of the army is on our side, my prince. They are prepared to fight to the death. Khalwyd, Silhas and Adlair will make their escape tonight. I will guide Khalwyd and Silhas here and we will complete the plan."

"And my uncle Adlair?"

"The people do not trust him. When he is gone it will be harder for Damon to convince them he is still manipulating you. Adlair will return to the mountains for a time."

"But I want to see him ..."

"That would be too dangerous, Eghan. He must be away, and quickly."

"This is it, isn't it, Ulhrik?" Eghan searched the old man's eyes. "This is the prophecy unfolding."

"Perhaps. We can only hold to the One True God and wait for Him to show us."

Eghan frowned. "I am not ready."

Ulhrik put a gnarled hand on Eghan's arm. "He will not ask of you what you cannot give. Nor will he allow it to happen before you are ready."

Eghan sighed and turned toward the window. A cold wind whistled through it. "And what of my father?"

"The king is in God's hands, as always."

Chapter Twenty-four

Malora flinched as her father raised his voice and cursed. "Find him! He could not have gone far."

"We have scoured the building," Rian said. "He is gone, brother, vanished. The guards say the wizard turned him into an eagle so he could fly from the tower." Malora's uncle seemed half in jest, half in awe. "There is no other way down from that height. The door was firmly bolted from the outside."

"Then he must have had help, you fool! Find out who it was and find the prince, and quickly. We cannot risk the people being roused."

As Rian turned to go, bellowing orders at the guards, Damon cursed again. He growled at the guards. "Double the guard on the wizard and the others. If he discovers they are alive, he will try to free them."

Malora watched the men scurry from the room. She was tempted to laugh but knew her father was in no mood to tolerate it. She watched him rave and pace about, staying as still as she could, trying to avoid his notice. As she watched him, she pondered again the feelings that stirred within her, unfamiliar feelings. But she did not try to push them away.

When she heard Eghan had escaped she had almost cried out with relief. It was a spontaneous reaction that had surprised her. Without him, their plans would be much more difficult, yet she was glad he was free.

If I could reach him, she thought, *perhaps I could persuade him ...*

Perhaps he would be willing to stand by her side so they could take control and be together.

Perhaps even now he is planning to join me.

She was roused from her fantasy by a renewed volley of curses, but they were not from her father. A soldier entered, dragging a servant with him.

The man cowered at Damon's feet as the guard explained the man had been one of their spies in the prince's chambers. Damon grabbed the front of his shirt and lifted him to his feet. "What can you tell me? Be quick."

The servant stammered. "I ... I ... we ...wwe...

The soldier struck the back of the man's head and bellowed, "speak!"

"We think he will head for Alinga territory, m'Lord. That's all, that's what we think he'll do."

Damon frowned down at him. "Why?"

"He was always pinin' after her, m'Lord, after the Alingan princess, even though she's been crowned queen of our natural born enemies, even though ..." The man's eyes flashed to Malora and went wide.

Malora reacted before she thought. Swiftly covering the distance between them, she raised her arm to strike, but her father caught her wrist before the blow could be landed. The smirk that slowly grew on his face made her stomach fill with bile. She wrenched her arm out of his grip.

"Jealousy does not become you, my dear. But it does tell me there may be some truth in this."

He released the man and spoke to the guard. "Send a battalion on the road into the mountains. Search every house. Question everyone. If he has fled that way, someone will have seen him."

The guard nodded, grabbed the boy's arm and pushed him toward the door.

Malora stood with her back to her father as she spoke. "He would not flee now. He knows his father and his friends are in danger."

Damon circled her. "Perhaps you give him credit for more loyalty than he possesses. Perhaps he will run for his life, run to the one he believes will help him, to the one he loves, that Alingan princess."

Malora strode away, keeping her back to her father, and lowered her voice until it was as cold and as hard as an edge of steel. "Then tell the guards, if they find him, to kill him on sight."

Damon took a quick step toward her, grasped her arm and turned her to face him. Then he brought the palm of his hand down hard across her face. "You are allowing emotion to interfere with our plans."

Malora dropped her eyes and raised her hand to her face. "Will you not allow me even to dream?"

"Dream? Yes, by all means, dream. Dream of

destroying the wench who stole power from our grasp when it was almost ours. Dream of controlling this valley as well as the mountain passes and the land beyond, as far as the sea, Malora! As far as the sea! Dream of being Queen over it all." His breath heated the tears that swelled in her eyes. "Dream of the power, not of some pitiful prince."

Chapter Twenty-five

Khalwyd leaped to his feet, his heart beating fast when he heard the guards coming. But when he saw Jhonar leading the soldiers toward their cell he almost smiled. At last, they were acting. He motioned to Silhas and Adlair to stay where they were, slumped down on the floor. He stepped deeper into the shadows of the cell and watched the men approach.

"Changing of the guard." Jhonar used his most authoritative voice.

Khalwyd noticed that some of the king's soldiers were dressed like Damon's men but their uniforms were incomplete. He prayed the dimness in the corridor would hide the lack. He was relieved to see Damon's men snap to attention, but their captain was peering at Jhonar suspiciously.

Jhonar did not give him time to wonder or to question. "As you can see, your Duke has strengthened our numbers, Captain. Relieve your men of their duty, but remind them to keep their eyes and ears open."

The captain hesitated only for a moment before

saluting and waving his men away from their posts. They paraded out of the corridor without incident.

Jhonar held up his hand when Silhas and Adlair stood, cautioning them to wait. Khalwyd counted the seconds until the last echo of the soldier's feet faded away. Finally Jhonar turned the key to their cell. No one spoke as the captain and his men hurried them along the corridors.

Ulhrik met them just before they emerged into the light. The old man pointed with his stick and the troop split off, the soldiers moving on into the outer courtyard, Adlair in their midst, while Khalwyd and the two other prisoners turned and began once again to descend. They had gone only a few paces when the stones in the floor disappeared and they dropped one by one through the hole into the darkness of a tunnel. It seemed interminable until a slit of light appeared ahead of them. Slowly it widened and climbed until it became a corridor again and Khalwyd knew they were in part of the house of prayer, their refuge, their fortress.

He almost gave a shout when he saw Eghan holding a torch and peering into the darkness. Khalwyd embraced him, sensing his relief.

"I thought you'd been hung," the prince said.

Khalwyd could not see his face clearly in the darkness but he knew by the sound of his voice the prince was nearly choking on his emotion.

"My neck is too stiff for any noose, Eghan. You should know that better than anyone."

"And mine is too slippery," Silhas said.

Khalwyd chuckled and slapped the prince's arm. "But let's find a deeper hole to hide in. This darkness seems to shape itself into enemies the more I peer into it."

Ulhrik stepped forward. "This way," he said. They went only a few more paces before the floor opened again.

Once in their hidden chamber, Khalwyd laid out the plan. At dawn, Eghan and Silhas and two selected men would make their way to the king's chambers. They would bring him here, by subduing him if necessary. At the same time, Khalwyd and Jhonar would mass as many men as possible and move against Damon. As soon as he and his men were driven from the valley, the king would be restored to his throne, with his son at his side.

The rest of that night was a sleepless one for Eghan. He peered into the darkness, his eyes wide open, trying to pray. He had never found it more difficult. The memory of the voice in his cell that had told him to trust had faded into a dream-like quality. He wondered now if it had been real, or if it was a delusion caused by lack of food and water.

He tried to focus on what God had already done. He had rescued him from a slow and torturous death. He had given Ulhrik enough time to finish his work, giving them a secure place to hide. And He had kept his friends alive, at least for now.

Eghan knew his uncle would soon be among the Hunstmen who would protect him. And in a few short hours his father would be beside him once again. Yes, God had done many amazing things for them all, but Eghan struggled to sense His presence with him right then, in the dark. A cold knot twisted inside him, a knot of doubt and fear. Malora's words kept ringing in his mind: "This time, you will lose everything." And another voice was getting stronger - a voice that hissed, "you will be abandoned by everyone, even by your God."

Eghan rolled onto his side and focused on the sounds of the men sleeping around him. What would he do if he were left so alone? He closed his eyes against the thought.

Before the light of dawn lit the window of their small sanctuary, the men were roused into full wakefulness. Ulhrik led Silhas and Eghan through silent tunnels and corridors until they recognized where they were. Two of the king's most trusted personal guard joined them as they entered the study that adjoined his private chambers.

Eghan was about to move to his father's bedroom when he heard low voices. He froze and motioned for the others to hide themselves. Taking care to move without sound, he took two more steps toward the door and jerked to a stop. Damon & Rian stood over the king, while a servant held a small lit taper. Rian reached down and touched Gherin's neck, then looked up, his face a contorted smirk in the light of the candle.

"The poison worked perfectly. He is dead."

Eghan felt Silhas' hand grip his arm. If the advisor feared that he would attack, he need not have worried. He was frozen where he stood, his mind reeling with the words he had just heard.

Damon's voice rose slightly. "See that he is laid out in his robes, with his sword and crown on his chest. The people must see that we honor their king. Malora will declare a time of mourning. And tell the guards to be alert. Perhaps this will bring the prince out of the hole where he has hidden himself."

They left the chamber quickly, throwing the men hidden in the shadows into total darkness.

Eghan remained where he was as Silhas stepped around him and approached the king's bed. He lit a lamp and bent over his face, listening for his breath. Hesitantly, he put a hand on the body. When Eghan saw his shoulders sag and begin to shake, he rushed forward, one word on his lips. "No."

Silhas's face was already wet when he turned to face the prince. "He is gone, Prince Eghan."

Eghan threw himself on his father's body and groaned. "No. Not like this. Not now."

He felt Silhas' hands grip his shoulders. "We must be away. Damon's men will act quickly. We must carry out the rest of the plan."

Eghan allowed himself to be pulled away. As they descended again into the dark lower regions of the castle and on, under the House of Prayer, he felt as though he were descending into his own grave.

Chapter Twenty-six

Malora stared at the black dress laid out for her.
She took a step toward it, feeling a terrible
weakness, as though what had been inside her was
dying. She was not aware that she was weeping
until her maid spoke.

"It is time, m'lady."

Malora nodded and wiped at her face. The girl
scooped the dress off the bed and approached.
Malora allowed the robe of mourning to be slipped
over her head, shivering as the black cloth touched
her skin. When her mourning dress was complete,
she dismissed the maid and peered into the long
glass that had so often puffed up her vanity. The
sight of the pale girl staring back at her now made
her cringe. Her knees gave out and she crumpled to
the floor, sobbing. Her mind filled with the image of
the king's face, the gentleness in his eyes when he
looked at her. Now that he was dead, Malora knew
no-one would ever look at her that way again. The
pain of that loss choked her until she gasped for
breath through her sobs. As she struggled for
control, she sensed a familiar presence. It hissed in

her ear, "He was a fool, who died a fool's death. The weak do not deserve to live." She put her hands over her ears, rocking back and forth.

"No," she moaned, "I do not want to listen."

The hissing continued, but she tried to block it out. Then she heard another voice, whispering. At first she could not understand, but slowly the words became clear.

"There is another who loves you, Malora, with a love much deeper than the king's."

The young woman sat up, every fiber of her being straining to hear that voice again. The whisper that escaped her own lips startled her, but as she spoke she felt strength returning.

"Their God," she whispered, "Eghan's God."

A searing pain forced her to the floor again. The hissing voice seemed to cut into her. "Lies! Their God is as weak as they are. Remember the plan. You will own it all, all will be yours!"

Gasping, Malora's mind suddenly cleared. She knew she no longer wanted the wealth and power, the revenge. She wanted love. Clutching her head, she spoke the words softly.

"I choose love." The pain became unbearable, but her voice was stronger. "I choose the One True God, Eghan's God." Writhing on the floor, she called out, "Please, God, help me!"

Instantly the pain was gone. She remained on the floor, her breathing slowly returning to normal. Then she felt as though she were on fire, but there was no pain, only a sense of wonder and joy and deep peace. She stood to her feet, swiftly placed the black mourning veil on her head, and draped it over her face. She left her chamber with a new and exhilarating resolve, heading for the place where King Gherin had been laid.

The soldiers surrounding the body moved aside as she entered the room. Seeing the king's body brought renewed tears to her eyes, but she did not waver from her purpose. She turned to the guards and spoke sharply.

"Leave me."

The captain frowned. "Leave, my lady? But..."

"You dare question my authority? Do you know who I am? I am now your Queen. Leave me!"

The soldiers bowed and made a quick exit.

Malora stepped closer to the body. She reached out and touched the man's cold cheek, whispering. "Oh, Your Majesty," she whispered, "if only I had had the courage to respond to your love while you yet lived." A sob escaped her and her shoulders shook. Then she heard voices in the corridor and was roused to her purpose. She reached for the sword of Lhin, taking it in both hands. As the voices drew nearer, she enfolded the weapon in her robes and fled from the room through the outer chambers.

****

Damon smiled as he saw his men driving the attackers back. He stood at a high rampart, watching, then turned to Rian and barked his orders. "Make sure the word is spreading that the king is dead from the wizard's poison. Tell them he still has Prince Eghan in his power. Stir their loyalty to their king - incite them to join us in the battle to restore the throne." As Rian left to carry out the plot, Damon's laughter rang out. "They will be so confused, brother will strike brother and a father his son. Chaos will rule."

****

Eghan's heart raced with the beat of the battle. Men swarmed around him, the sound of curses and screams of pain filling his ears. He could not tell if they were gaining ground or losing it. Khalwyd stayed at his side and more than once stood in the way of blows intended to strike him. Damon's men fought with the fury of demons. It seemed as though they had been in the battle for days, when Khalwyd suddenly turned to him, gripped his arm and shouted in his ear.

"Fall back, we must re-group."

As they retreated, a deadening weariness seemed to lie heavily on Eghan and those with him. Within the safety of the House of Prayer, they counted their casualties and sat in counsel. Many had been lost, but surrender was never considered. Silhas and Khalwyd laid out the next plan of attack and drew the men together to pray. In spite of the prayers,

Eghan's heart filled with foreboding. As they were about to charge out of the house, they heard the roar of an army coming against them. Khalwyd stood at the doors and turned to face the men.

"Fight bravely. Whatever the result, know our God reigns." He raised his sword and led the charge.

Eghan lost sight of him immediately as men swarmed against them. For a time they seemed to make headway, forcing the opposers back, but then confusion reigned. Eghan heard men scream in the name of his father as they slew his father's guards. Those who had been loyal stood in the ranks of Damon's army. Eghan continually called out, trying to rally those who were close enough to hear, but few responded. Those who did were quickly slain.

Silhas was at his side, urging him to pull back. "They are too strong, Prince Eghan. You must save yourself. If you die, the kingdom dies with you."

Eghan turned to him in time to see a spear pierce his body. As he fell to the ground, the king's loyal adviser grasped Eghan's leg and begged him to retreat. Eghan had time to neither respond nor grieve. He raised his sword just in time to deflect a blow and threw himself into the battle.

He was on the outer edge of the mass of men when he heard a woman's voice calling his name. At first he ignored it, but the sound grew more distinct as he moved back toward the doors of the House of Prayer. Silhas's entreaty ringing in his mind, he fought his way toward them. One of his father's own soldiers fell to his sword as he reached the steps and looked up. The shock of what he saw there almost caused him to drop his weapon.

A woman in black stood before the doors, the sword of Lhin in her hands. As he stared, she raised the weapon high and beckoned to him. He started toward her, but his way was blocked by two of Damon's guards. They leered at him as they charged. Behind them, Eghan saw the woman fall. The sword of Lhin vanished from his sight.

The two soldiers seemed empowered by the devil himself. Eghan fell back time and again under the blows of their weapons. He was weakening badly, when one of his father's soldiers joined him, engaging one of the attackers. The other came on with renewed force, narrowly missing his mark time after time as Eghan fought for his life. He was almost to the top of the stairs when the soldier's sword sliced deeply into his arm. Eghan fell back, moaning, and clutched at the wound, his weapon clanging on the stone as it fell from his hand. Expecting to see the man posing for the kill, Eghan looked up, but Khalwyd was suddenly there, his sword flashing. Eghan crawled up the few stairs to where the woman in black lay. He gently turned her onto her side and lifted the veil. Malora's golden hair was matted with blood. She moaned and opened her eyes.

"Eghan. Please, forgive me."

He touched her cheek. As the last of her breath seeped away, she smiled.

Tears streaming, Eghan took his father's sword from her hands. It now truly belonged to him. He forced himself to his feet before the doors of the House of Prayer. The sword of the House of Lhin was in his hand, but all around him was fire and smoke. The smell of death made him stagger. He looked down at his arm. Blood ran freely from it. Khalwyd reached him just as he sank to the stone. He felt Khalwyd's hands lift him and tried to raise himself as he was dragged into the sanctuary.

Eghan shook his head, trying to gain his feet, but the world spun around him. The sounds of battle faded into a far-off roar. As Khalwyd lowered him to the floor, Eghan looked into his guardian's face. Blood seeped from a gash on his friend's forehead. Their eyes locked and Eghan knew what he intended. With all the strength left in him, he threw himself on Khalwyd's arm.

"No!"

His guardian pried his hands away and staggered to his feet. Eghan saw a thin shadow bend over him and heard a voice as though through a long tunnel.

"They are upon us. You must keep them at bay, Khalwyd, until we reach the lower chambers. Go!"

Eghan moaned and slipped into darkness.

Chapter Twenty-seven

Nara lifted her head and stopped praying as Burke hurried into her chambers.

"My lady?" He knelt on one knee beside her. "What is it?"

"Something terrible has happened, Burke. I have sensed it, just as I did the day Dulah died. I have been praying but can find no relief. We must send a messenger immediately." She gripped Burke's hands. "I must know what has happened in the Valley of Lhin before leaving for Brimladin Ula."

Burke frowned. "But there is not enough time, my lady. Our fastest messenger could not get to the Valley of Lhin and back within the week and you must be well on your way before then."

Nara stood and paced. "I will send my regrets to King Delmar and hope that he will allow me to visit another time."

Burke shook his head. "I don't advise you to do that, my lady. From what I have learned of this king, he does not suffer such slights well. And we cannot afford to risk that he may become an adversary."

Nara flung out her hands. "But how can I leave when I am so certain disaster is at our door?"

Burke took her hands. "We must continue to pray and trust in The One True God to show us what to do. We must pray until peace, and an answer, comes"

Nara nodded. "Gather our prayer warriors, Burke."

She watched him stride from the room, then sank down to her knees.

It was not long before Brynna brought word that a prayer vigil had been struck and the people had gathered. Nara stepped onto the balcony of her chambers and was stunned at what she saw. The courtyard was full of men and women on their knees.

"There are more gathering in the villages, my lady," Brynna said. It is a mighty army of prayer warriors."

Nara could not keep the tears from streaming from her face. She turned back into her room. "Bring my cloak, Brynna. I will join them."

No one took notice as Nara slipped into the courtyard and joined her people on her knees. For a time she listened as the prayers were spoken, some loud and authoritative, some soft and pleading. Then Nara bowed her head to the cobblestones and prayed.

She became aware of the silence after some time and raised her head. The people were watching her. She stood as Burke came to her side and took her arm to lead her back into the house. At the doorway Nara turned and smiled at her people.

"Thank you," she said. "The Lord has answered. He is sovereign over all and whatever comes, He will be with us."

As she entered the house Burke spoke quietly to the servants, telling them to prepare for their departure the next day.

Chapter Twenty-eight

Ulhrik's lips moved in prayer as he sponged the prince's fevered face with a cold cloth.

"Is 'e goin t' live, Master Ulhrik?"

"The Lord is in control of life and death, Latham. Eghan is in God's hands."

The boy stared at the blood-soaked tunic they had torn from the prince's body. "So much blood," he murmured.

Ulhrik nodded. "The wound is deep, but the cauterizing has stopped the flow."

Latham made a face and Ulhrik knew he was remembering the smell of burning flesh. The boy squatted beside his young master as Ulhrik turned to bathe his face again. His lips continued to move in prayer. When he turned to rinse the cloth in the basin Latham held, the boy peered into his face and spoke hesitantly.

"I ... I want to pray too."

Ulhrik's voice quavered with emotion. "The Father is always approachable, Latham, by anyone who has accepted the Son."

Latham nodded. "Prince Eghan told me about

Him, but I ... I'm just a servant, Master Ulhrik."

"So are we all, my boy. Pray. He will listen."

Latham glanced down at the prince and whispered, "Please, don't let 'im die."

****

It was three more days before the fever broke and another night before Eghan opened his eyes. When he did, he tried to speak, but Ulhrik would not allow it. He held Eghan's head and spooned a dark broth into his mouth.

"You have lost a great deal of blood, Eghan. You must be still."

Eghan did not have the will nor the energy to argue. For several days he raised his head only to drink the broth or water. His eyes never seemed to focus. Latham was at his side when he spoke, weakly, for the first time.

"I must speak to my father."

Latham's mouth opened but no words came out.

Eghan tried to raise himself. "Do you hear, boy?"

"Oh my yes, m'lord, I hear ye. But lay still, m'Lord. Ulhrik's just gone fer food. He'll be back soon, m'Lord."

Eghan frowned. "Ulhrik?"

"He'll be here soon, m'Lord."

"Where is Khalwyd?"

Before Latham could answer, Eghan groaned and lay back. "My arm."

"It's healin'm'Lord, but you must lie still."

Eghan peered at him and the pain in the boy's eyes made him cringe.

"I have had such dreams, Latham … or … were they dreams?"

"Shhh. Please, m'Lord. Don't talk."

"My Father's sword …" Eghan tried to sit up again, but groaned and fell back.

Latham leaned over him, seeming eager to give at least some good news. "The sword of Lhin is here, m'Lord, it's safe with us."

"Good." Eghan nodded. "Good." Exhausted by the effort, he lay back and let the darkness take him again.

When he woke again he heard a low mumble of voices. Opening his eyes, darkness surrounded him and fear seared him like a fire.

"Who is there?"

The light of a torch hovered above him and Ulhrik's voice was strong. "Your servants, Sire."

Eghan did not miss the significance of the words. The vague dreams came rushing into focus. He lay back and was silent as Ulhrik sat beside him. When Eghan spoke again, the words were barely a whisper. "They are all dead, Ulhrik?"

The old man did not answer, but only laid his hand on Eghan's chest. Eghan allowed it to rest there for a moment, then rolled away onto his side and put his face against the cold stone wall. Sobs racked his body until exhaustion once again swallowed him in darkness.

When the young king was still, Ulhrik turned back to the boy crouched against the wall. "Do you understand the plan, Latham?"

The boy nodded his tear stained face. "Aye, m'Lord. I will bring the cart at daybreak."

"Be sure no one sees you. If you are recognized..."

"I will keep myself hidden. But ... is 'e strong enough yet, m'Lord? Should we not wait?"

Ulhrik shook his head. "We cannot risk remaining here any longer. We are sure to be seen as we venture out for food and water. If he is left alone now he will die. We must take him to a safer place."

Latham nodded but shivered with fear. "Will anywhere be safe?" he mumbled.

Ulhrik put a hand on his arm. "Go," he said.

Latham shook himself and stood. "I'll bring the cart, Master Ulhrik, but you'll have t' show me the way out."

Ulhrik looked down at Eghan. He was reluctant, but agreed. "Come, then, while he sleeps."

****

Eghan woke to utter darkness. No glimmer of light softened it, no hope relieved his pain. In a sudden surge of anger, he cried out. "Where is your mercy now? Where is your justice? Your promises mean nothing. Nothing!"

The last word echoed back from the stone. Eghan slammed his fist against the floor and wept until sleep overcame him. The room began to glow. The pain was gone and the sweet smell of perfume made him smile. Malora bent over him, her eyes full of concern. Her cheek touched his as she leaned toward him. He closed his eyes at the softness of it, until her words rang in his ear.

"Curse him, Eghan. Free yourself from your god and come with me."

Eghan pushed her away. "No. No, I could never curse Him. Never."

Malora's face began to change. Her body shriveled into a hideous black shape. Her voice became a serpent's hiss.

"You fool! You have cursed him. And he has abandoned you. You belong to me!"

The creature grew before Eghan's eyes until it filled the room. As he watched, Eghan knew it had spoken the truth. He had cursed God. A pressure began to build on his chest, a weight squeezing the breath from his lungs. He tried to raise himself against it but could not. The voice hissed at him from every direction. "Deny your Christ and live! Deny Him! Deny Him!"

In total weakness, Eghan murmured, "I belong to Him." His voice gaining strength, he spoke again. "Father, I belong only to You. Forgive my weakness. Take my life if you will, only forgive me!"

With a blood curdling scream, the creature writhed in the air and vanished. Eghan woke, panting. Pain from his arm pulsed through him like the rhythmic beat of a drum, and fear kept pace with it.

When Ulhrik returned the relief in his voice was plain. "I hoped you would be awake. Latham is bringing a cart to the end of a hidden passageway at dawn. God willing, we will be well away before most are stirring from their beds. It is some distance to where Latham will be waiting. If we start now, you can rest, as you need, along the way."

Eghan did not resist as the old man wrapped a blanket around him and helped him stand. They had not gone far when Eghan's weakness made them stop. It seemed to take the entire night to reach the place, but finally they came to a long stairway opening into a narrow alley. They did not have long to wait before Latham appeared, pulling a small cart.

Eghan moaned as he crawled under a filthy hide. Within minutes he felt the cart jerk as Ulhrik pulled a rope sling over his shoulder and nodded to Latham. Without a word, the two dragged the cart forward, bearing the king of the House of Lhin out of his own kingdom.

The End

If you have enjoyed this book please consider
posting a review on Amazon

Continue to follow Prince Eghan's journey. Will his
kingdom be lost to him forever?

Read Book 3 in the Higher Ways Series,
Journey to a New Beginning, available on Amazon.

Manufactured by Amazon.ca
Bolton, ON